VALERIA LUISELLI was born in Mexico City. Her work has been published in the *New York Times*, *McSweeney's*, *Dazed & Confused* and *Granta*, and has been translated into many languages. She is also the author of the novel *Faces in the Crowd* and a collection of essays, *Sidewalks*. She lives in New York City.

CHRISTINA MACSWEENEY has an MA in Literary Translation from the University of East Anglia. As well as her acclaimed translations of Valeria Luiselli, she has published translations on platforms including *Granta* online, *Words without Borders*, *McSweeney's*, *Quarterly Conversation*, *A Public Space* and the anthology *México 20*. Her latest translation is of *Among Strange Victims* by Daniel Saldaña París.

'Luiselli follows in the imaginative tradition of writers like Borges and Márquez, but her style and concerns are unmistakably her own … She has become a writer to watch, in part because it's truly hard to know (but exciting to wonder about) where she will go next' *New York Times*

'This giddy, witty, idiosyncratic novel … is a jubilant celebration of the act of storytelling … Luiselli persuasively suggests that our lives would be empty vessels, hardly worth bidding on, without the "stories that give them value and meaning"' *Wall Street Journal*

'Proof that Luiselli is one of the most exciting new writers working today' *Los Angeles Times*

'Quirky and charming … a delightful meditation on art, value, and truth' *BuzzFeed*

'A playful, philosophical funhouse of a read that demonstrates that not only isn't experimental fiction dead, it needn't be deadly, either' *NPR*

'Although buoyant, Luiselli's work never seems flippant, perhaps because of her precise prose style … Linear at first glance, it soon opens out into a world of stories, like a mouth with one tooth from every artist in the world' *Chicago Tribune*

'Confident, playful, learned … translated into utterly convincing English via Luiselli's collaboration with Christina MacSweeney' *Times Literary Supplement*

Also by Valeria Luiselli

Faces in the Crowd
Sidewalks

The Story
of My Teeth

VALERIA LUISELLI

Translated by Christina MacSweeney

GRANTA

Granta Publications, 12 Addison Avenue, London W11 4QR

First published in Great Britain by Granta Books, 2015
This paperback edition published by Granta Books, 2016
First published in the USA by Coffee House Press, 2015

Offset by Avon DataSet Ltd, Bidford on Avon, Warwickshire

Printed and bound by CPI Group (UK) Ltd, Croydon, CR0 4YY

www.grantabooks.com

MIX
Paper from
responsible sources
FSC® C020471

FOR THE JUMEX FACTORY STAFF

BOOK I

The Story
(Beginning, Middle, and End)

A man may have been named John because that was the name of his father; a town may have been named Dartmouth, because it is situated at the mouth of the Dart. But it is no part of the signification of the word John, that the father of the person so called bore the same name; nor even of the word Dartmouth, to be situated at the mouth of the Dart.

—J. S. MILL

I'M THE BEST AUCTIONEER IN THE WORLD, BUT NO ONE knows it because I'm a discreet sort of man. My name is Gustavo Sánchez Sánchez, though people call me Highway, I believe with affection. I can imitate Janis Joplin after two rums. I can interpret Chinese fortune cookies. I can stand an egg upright on a table, the way Christopher Columbus did in the famous anecdote. I know how to count to eight in Japanese: ichi, ni, san, shi, go, roku, shichi, hachi. I can float on my back.

This is the story of my teeth, and my treatise on collectibles and the variable value of objects. As any other story, this one begins with the Beginning; and then comes the Middle, and then the End. The rest, as a friend of mine always says, is literature: hyperbolics, parabolics, circulars, allegorics, and elliptics. I don't know what comes after that. Possibly ignominy, death, and, finally, postmortem fame. At that point it will no longer be my place to say anything in the first person. I will be a dead man, a happy, enviable man.

Some have luck, some have charisma. I've got a bit of both. My uncle, Solón Sánchez Fuentes, a salesman dealing in quality Italian ties, used to say that beauty, power, and early success fade away, and that they're a heavy burden for those who possess them, because the prospect of their loss is a threat few can endure. I've never had to worry about that, because there's nothing ephemeral in my nature. I have only permanent qualities. I inherited every last jot of my uncle Solón's charisma, and he also left me an elegant Italian tie. That's all you need in this life to become a man of pedigree, he said.

I was born in Pachuca, the Beautiful Windy City, with four premature teeth and my body completely covered in a very fine coat of fuzz. But I'm grateful for that inauspicious start, because ugliness, as my other uncle, Eurípides López Sánchez, was given to saying, is character forming. When my father first saw me, he claimed his real son had been taken away by the new mother in the next room. He tried by various means—bureaucracy, blackmail, intimidation—to return me to the nurse who had handed me over. But Mom took me in her arms the moment she saw me: a tiny, brown, swollen blob fish. She had been trained to accept filth as her fate. Dad hadn't.

The nurse explained to my parents that the presence of my four teeth was a rare condition in our country, but one that was not uncommon among other races. It was called congenital prenatal dentition.

What kind of races? asked my father, on the defensive.

Caucasians, sir, said the nurse.

But this child is as dark as the inside of a needle, Dad replied.

Genetics is a science full of gods, Mr. Sánchez.

That must have consoled my father. He finally resigned himself to carrying me home in his arms, wrapped up in a thick flannel blanket.

Not long after my birth, we moved to Ecatepec, where Mom made a living cleaning other people's houses. Dad didn't clean anything, not even his own nails. They were thick, rough, and black. He used to pare them with his teeth. Not from anxiety, but because he was idle and overbearing. While I was doing my homework at the table, he would be silently studying them, stretched out by the fan in the green velvet armchair Mom inherited from Mr. Cortázar, our neighbor in 4-A, after he died of tetanus. When Mr. Cortázar's progeny came to take away his belongings, they left us his macaw, Criteria—who suffered a terminal case of sadness after a few weeks—and the green velvet armchair where Dad took to lounging every evening. Lost to the world, he would study the damp patches on the ceiling while listening to public radio and pull off pieces of nail, one finger at a time.

Starting with his little finger, he'd press a corner of the nail between his upper and lower central incisors, detach a tiny sliver, and, in a single motion, tear off the half moon of excess nail. After he'd detached the sliver, he'd hold it in his mouth for a moment or two, roll his tongue, and blow: it would shoot out and land on the notebook I was using to do my homework. The dogs would be barking outside in the street. I'd contemplate the piece of nail lying there, dead and dirty, a few millimeters from the point of my pencil. Then I'd draw a circle around it and go on doing my writing exercises, carefully avoiding the circle. Bits of nail would keep falling from the heavens onto my ruled Scribe notebook like meteorites propelled by the current of air from the fan: ring, middle, index, and, finally, the thumb. And then the other hand. I'd go on fitting the letters around the small circumferenced craters left on the page by Dad's airborne trash. When I was finished, I'd gather up the nails into a small pile and put them in my trouser pocket. Afterward, in my bedroom, I'd place them in a paper envelope I kept under my pillow. During the course of my childhood, the nail collection got to be so large that I filled several envelopes. End of memory.

Dad no longer has any teeth. Or nails, or a face: he was cremated two years ago, and, at his request, Mom and I scattered his ashes in Acapulco Bay. A year later, I buried Mom next to her sisters and brothers in Pachuca, the Beautiful Windy City. It's always raining there, and there's hardly a breath of air. I travel to Pachuca to see her once a month, usually on Sundays. But I never go as far as the cemetery, because I'm allergic to pollen and there are lots of flowers there. I get off the bus not far from the gates, at a lovely median strip with life-size dinosaur sculptures, and I stay right there among the gentle fiberglass beasts—getting soaked, saying Our Fathers—until my feet swell up and I feel tired. Then I go back across the street, carefully dodging the puddles—round as the craters in my childhood notebook—and wait for the bus to take me back to the station.

My first job was at the Rubén Darío newspaper stand, on the corner of Aceites and Metales. I was eight years old and all my milk teeth had already fallen out. They had been replaced by others, as wide as shovels, each pointing in a different direction. My boss's wife, Azul, was my first true friend, even though she was twenty years older than me. Her husband kept her locked up in the house. At eleven every morning, he sent me there with a set of keys to see what Azul was doing and to ask if I could fetch her anything from the shops.

Azul would generally be lying on the bed in her underwear, with Mr. Unamuno all over her. Mr. Unamuno was a pigeon-chested old codger who had a program on public radio. His show always opened with the same line: "This is Unamuno: modestly depressed, engagingly eclectic, and sentimentally political." Idiot. When I came into the room, Mr. Unamuno would spring up, tuck in his shirt, and clumsily button up his trousers. I, in the meanwhile, would be looking at the floor and, sometimes, out of the corner of my eye, at Azul, who would still be lying on the bed, staring at the ceiling, passing the tips of her fingers over her bared midriff.

When he was finally fully dressed and with his glasses on, Mr. Unamuno would come over and give me a rap on the forehead with the palm of his hand.

Weren't you taught to knock, Turnpike?

Azul used to come to my defense: He's called Highway, and he's my friend. And then she'd give a deep and simple laugh, showing disconcertingly long canine teeth with flattened points.

After Mr. Unamuno had finally slipped out—all anxious—through the back door, Azul would wrap the sheet around herself like a superhero's cape and invite me to jump on the bed. When we got tired of jumping, we'd lie down and play pocket billiards. She was always very gentle. When we'd finished that, she'd give me a slice of bread and a pouch of mineral water with a straw, then send me back to the newspaper stand. On the way, I'd drink the water and put the straw in my pocket for later. I eventually accumulated more than ten thousand straws, word of honor.

What was Azul doing? Mr. Darío would ask when I returned to the stand.

I'd cover for her, inventing the details of some innocent activity:

She was just trying to thread a needle to mend her cousin's new baby's christening gown.

Which cousin?

She didn't say.

It must be Sandra, or Berta. Here's your tip, and now off to school with you.

I finished primary, middle, and high school and passed unnoticed with good grades, because I'm the sort that doesn't make waves. I never opened my mouth, not even to answer at roll call. My silence wasn't for fear of them seeing my crooked teeth, but because I'm a discreet sort. I learned many things at school. End of beginning.

At the age of twenty-one, I was offered a job as a security guard in a factory on Vía Morelos, due to that selfsame discretion, I believe. The factory produced juices. And the juices, in turn, produced art. That is to say, the profits from the juice sales funded the largest art collection in the continent. It was a good job to have since, although I was only in charge of guarding the factory entrance and was never allowed into the gallery where the art was shown, I was in a sense the gatekeeper of a collection of objects of real beauty and truth. I worked there for nineteen years. Setting aside six months when I was off sick with hepatitis, three days for an ominous case of tooth decay that ended up needing a double root canal treatment, and my annual leave, I spent exactly eighteen years and three months as a factory security guard. They weren't bad years, but they weren't good either.

But one day Fortuna spun her wheel, as Napoleón, the singer, says. On the very day of my fortieth birthday, the Pasteurization Operator got a panic attack while he was attending to a DHL messenger, a plump man of medium height. The Polymer Supervisor's Secretary had never witnessed a panic attack before and thought the messenger of medium height was assaulting the Pasteurization Operator, because her workmate had put his hands to his throat, gone purple as a plum, turned his eyes up, and let himself fall backwards, collapsing spread-eagled on the floor.

The Customer Services Manager ordered me to apprehend the messenger of medium height. Following his command, I made straight for the suspected criminal. My old friend and workmate, El Perro, one of the factory drivers, was just coming in through the door; he ran toward us and helped me to pin the messenger of medium height down. But when I then hit the messenger at the base of his spine with the tip of my truncheon—not even very hard—he started to cry inconsolably. El Perro let him go, of course, because he's not a sadistic type. While I was hustling the messenger to the exit, I asked, in a more gentle tone, for his ID. With one hand raised high, he put the other in his pocket and took out his wallet. Then, with the raised hand, he extracted his driver's license and handed it to me, unable to look me straight in the eyes: Avelino Lisper—a ridiculous name. The Customer Services Manager told me to go back immediately to help my moribund companion, because he was still lying on the floor and couldn't breathe. I told the messenger of medium height that he could go—though, in fact, what he did was to just stand there crying, bathed in tears you might say—and ran to the Pasteurization Operator, using the tip of my truncheon to clear a path through the curious onlookers. I knelt down by him, took him in my arms, and, for want of a better solution, silently cradled him until the attack had passed. El Perro, in the meantime, had to comfort the DHL messenger until he too calmed down.

The next day, the Manager called me into his office and told me that I was going to be promoted.

Guards are second class, he explained to me in private, and you're a first-class man.

The Senior Executives had decided that, from then on, I would have a chair and a desk of my own, and my job would consist of comforting any member of staff who required this service.

You're going to be our Personnel Crisis Supervisor, said the Manager, with the slightly sinister smile of those who have paid many visits to the dentist.

Two weeks went by, and, as the Pasteurization Operator was on temporary leave of absence, there was no one in need of comforting. The factory had employed a new guard: a fat, overeager little lovemedo sort of guy who went by the name of Hochimin and spent the whole day trying to chat with people. Discretion is a quality that few people appreciate. I eyed him condescendingly from my new position. I'd been given an adjustable swivel chair and a desk with a drawer containing a divine assortment of rubber bands and paperclips. Every day, I'd put one of each in my trouser pocket and take them home. I managed to build up a good collection.

But it wasn't all velvet petals and marshmallow clouds, as Napoleón says. Some employees at the factory, particularly the Customer Services Manager, began to complain that I was now being paid to bite my nails and look at the ceiling. Some of them even hatched a conspiracy theory according to which the Pasteurization Operator and I had worked out the little scam so that he'd be given a month's paid sick leave and I'd get promoted—typical cock-and-bull stories and skullduggery of miserable wretches who can't deal with other people's good fortune. After a general meeting, the Manager arranged for me to be sent on specialized courses, to keep me busy while, incidentally, acquiring the skills needed for managing possible crises among the staff.

I began to travel. I became a man of the world. I attended seminars and participated in workshops the length and breadth of the Republic, even the Continent. You could say that I became a collector of courses: First Aid, Anxiety

Control, Nutrition and Dietary Habits, Listening and Assertive Communication, DOS, New Masculinities, Neurolinguistics. That was a golden age. Until it all came to an end, like everything glorious and good. The beginning of the end started with a course I had to take in the Department of Philosophy and Letters of the National University. It was given by the Manager's son, so I couldn't refuse without putting my job at risk. I accepted. The course was called—to my horror, shame, and consternation—"Contact-Improv Dance."

The first exercise in the workshop involved inventing a dance routine, in pairs. My partner turned out to be a certain Flaca, who, though indeed thin, was neither pretty nor ugly. This Flaca used me as a pole, dancing around me in the style of that curvaceous, exotic artiste of the sixties, Tongolele, while I just snapped my fingers, trying to follow the difficult rhythm of the song, which she totally disregarded. She slid her hands over my body, ran her fingers through my hair, undid buttons. I continued snapping my fingers conscientiously. By the time the song had finished, Flaca's femininity was in full bloom and I was deflowered, converted into a contact-improv dancer, standing half naked on a parquet-floored stage in the Department of Philosophy and Letters, my balls the size of two tadpoles. End of memory.

To save face, I had no choice but to marry Flaca a few months later. Et cetera, et cetera, and she got pregnant. I left my job in the juice factory, because she thought I had a real talent for dance and possibly theater, and shouldn't waste any more time. I became her personal project, her social service, her contribution to the nation. Flaca was brought up in an all-girl Catholic school, and was as perverted as any of those rich white Mexican girls. But she had rebelled, or so she said, and was studying to become a Buddhist. As she had saved enough from her earnings—lies: it was her father's money—she offered to support me if the dance-theater thing didn't turn out to be particularly remunerative. I was ready to go along with that. I moved into her oversized apartment in Polanco and lived the life of a prince. Then, as always happens, after a pretty short time, Flaca got fat.

For all the élan I put into it, and despite the material perfection of my corporality, I couldn't find work as a contemporary dancer or actor. I auditioned for the Icarus Fallen Dance Company, for Alternative Dimension, Cosmic Race, and even the Open Space group, which, as its name suggests, is very open and accepts anyone. Nothing. I was almost accepted by FolkArt, but in the end a shorty with the body of a shrimp and the ridiculously pretentious name of Brendy got the spot.

For a while I went around, as Napoleón says, like green wood that won't burn and a tree that doesn't put down roots. Flaca decided I had to cultivate myself, so she forced me to sit in on Classical Philology and Modern Literature lectures at the National University. At first I loathed the classroom life, but I grew into it, I believe because I am a flexible man. If I was going to be a father, I told myself, I'd need to be able to tell my son or daughter stories. I don't know if I was a good student, since they never gave me grades, but it at least got me reading. I didn't take to the novelists, but I did like some poets and certainly all the essayists: Mr. Michel de Montaigne, Mr. Rousseau, Mr. Chesterton, Mrs. Woolf. More than anything, however, I loved the classics. I read them from the first page to the last, word of honor. My favorite is Gaius Suetonius Tranquillus, whose *The Twelve Caesars* I still consult, oracle-wise, every night before going to sleep.

Once in bed, the blankets pulled up to my chest, I reach with my right hand under the pillow and draw out the book—the way a cowboy would draw a pistol from under his pillow, but a bit more slowly. Then I close my eyes and, using both hands, open the book and raise it above my head, letting its pages dangle above me. Then I slowly bring it closer to my face, until my nose touches the edge of the pages and slides between two of them. Those are the pages I read. I often write the date on which I read them in the margin with a little note. On August 16, 1985, for example, I wrote, "I will be like Octavius Augustus when I am older," and underlined the paragraph I had read:

His teeth were small, few and decayed [...] his eyebrows met above his nose; he had ears of normal size, a nose was prominent at the bridge and curved downward at the tip, and a complexion intermediate between dark and fair [...] His body is said to have been marred by blemishes of various sorts—a constellation of seven birthmarks on his chest and stomach, exactly corresponding with the Great Bear, and a number of hard, dry patches suggesting ringworm, caused by an itching of his skin and a too vigorous use of the scraper at the baths ...

On September 19, 1985, there was a strong earthquake in Mexico City, as had been predicted by Julián Herbert, the astrologer in *Diario Ecatepec*. A few minutes afterward, Siddhartha Sánchez Tostado was born. That's what Flaca called our son. I, for my part, liked the name Yoko, since I always had been keen on Japanese culture and the Beatles. But as the child was a boy, I had to accept Flaca's choice. We'd agreed on that. Siddhartha was born healthy, without any distinguishing features. I won't say that he was a pretty baby, but neither was he ugly. End of comment.

When Siddhartha was beginning to crawl and Flaca had finally gotten over her postpartum depression, I invited my friend El Perro to dinner. The evening had been going well, and we'd been recalling the old times with nostalgia until Flaca served the coffee, and El Perro told me that a few days earlier, he'd run into Hochimin, the replacement guard who chatted too much. He'd seen him in a cantina wearing an expensive suit and in distinguished company.

How did he do it? I asked.

He became an auctioneer, he said.

Just like that? I asked, struggling to swallow my coffee.

El Perro explained. It seems that what had happened was that when I left my job in the factory, Hochimin asked the Manager for permission to take a training course in case of a crisis among the staff. I believe he did this because he wanted to be like me. They only sent him on one course, for

First Aid, but the shameless trickster made use of the free time to enroll in an auctioneering course in Mexico City's Korean neighborhood, in the Zona Rosa. A month later, he gave up his job at the factory and began auctioning cars. He was doing well. Better than the rest of us put together, El Perro said.

The next day, I took the metro to the Korean neighborhood and walked the streets in search of announcements for auctions, auctioneers, or anything at all related. After hours of fruitless searching and with my soul racked by hunger, I went into a restaurant and ordered kimchi, the specialty of the house. In one corner of the restaurant, a ghostly youth was playing the guitar and singing a catchy sort of tune about a man who lost sight of a woman in the Balderas metro station.

I started leafing through a newspaper, trying to keep at bay the implacable gusts of melancholy that assail you when you don't eat your meals at normal times. I had taken to reading the newspaper right through, particularly when I was sunk in the self-pity engendered by my repeated rejections in the world of dance and theater. Other people's misery and other people's fortune always puts my own into perspective. I read a story that day in the newspaper about a certain local writer who had had all his teeth replaced. This writer, apparently, was able to afford the new dentures and the expensive operation because he'd written a novel. A novel! I saw my future, crystal clear. If that writer had had his teeth fixed with a book, I could do it too. Or, even better, I could get someone to write one for me. I cut out the article and put it in my wallet. I still keep it with me at all times, as a talisman.

As I've already said, I am a lucky man. When I'd finished eating and was walking toward the door to leave the restaurant, my eyes came to rest on a notice taped to one of the walls. In neat handwriting, the appeal to my destiny read: "Learn the art of auctioneering. Success guaranteed. Yushimito Method." While the waitress was preparing my check, I copied the address on a napkin.

The intensive initiation course into the art of auctioneering lasted a month and took place every evening from three to nine in the back room of Hair Charisma, a Japanese-Korean barber's shop in Calle Londres. The teacher—Japanese by origin—went by the name of Master Oklahoma, because he'd studied auctioneering there. His real name was Kenta Yushimito, and his Western name Carlos Yushimito. He was a man of great breadth of mind, elegance, and distinction; the living embodiment of discretion.

My characteristic awareness of what is seemly, as well as my loyalty to and respect for both my teacher and our profession, prevent me from revealing the secrets of the art of auctioneering. But there is one thing I can explain about the Yushimito Method, which derives from a combination of classical rhetoric and the mathematical theory of eccentricity. According to Master Oklahoma, there are four types of auctions: circular, elliptical, parabolic, and hyperbolic. The strand that any auction follows is, in turn, determined by the relative value of the eccentricity (epsilon) of the auctioneer's discourse; that is to say, the degree of deviation of its conic section from a given circumference (the object to be auctioned). The range of values is as follows:

THE EPSILON OF THE CIRCULAR METHOD IS ZERO.
THE EPSILON OF THE ELLIPTICAL METHOD IS GREATER THAN
ZERO BUT LESS THAN ONE.
THE EPSILON OF THE PARABOLIC METHOD IS ONE.
THE EPSILON OF THE HYPERBOLIC METHOD IS GREATER
THAN ONE.

With the passage of time, I developed and added another category to Master Oklahoma's auctioning methods, although I didn't put it into practice until many years later. This was the allegoric method, the eccentricity (epsilon) of which is infinite and does not depend on contingent or material variables. I am sure that my master would have approved.

During our first meeting, Master Oklahoma sat before us in a hairdresser's chair and, in order to demonstrate the parabolic method, auctioned a pair of scissors. He successfully sold them by telling a short, simple story about their origins. Despite the fact that we were all there, sitting in front of him, notebooks and pencils in hand, fully aware that we were his students and not a group of buyers of any variety, since we had already shelled out the exorbitant price of the course, our grandmaster took the pair of scissors from the counter and worked on us until one student, Mr. Morato, pulled out his wallet and paid 750 pesos for it.

The most important thing in this life, Master Oklahoma used to say at the end of each session, is to have a destiny.

He would scan our faces with an expression that gave nothing away and the barest insinuation of a smile. Then we'd count to eight in Japanese, breathing deeply, with our eyes closed, and the session would be over. We'd reverently take our leave of him and our fellow students with a nod of the head.

I had a clear goal, a destiny: I was going to become an auctioneer in order to have my teeth fixed, like that writer did with his book. More importantly, I was going to have them fixed so I could leave Flaca, who was always going to be fat and ill natured. And after that, so I could marry someone else—perhaps Vanesa or María or Verónica, the three most attractive students in the course.

Flaca had become mentally abusive. She used to make me pee sitting down because, otherwise, I splashed; she'd send me away to sleep in a chair because I snored; I was banned from walking barefoot because my feet sweated and left prints on the floor. She had developed issues with me, because she was the provider and I the consumer. When she got mad, she called me Gustabo or sometimes Gustapo or even Gestapo. At nights, when I couldn't sleep, I used to imagine Vanesa calling me Beefcake; María, Gamecock; Verónica, Himbo. Restless, wide awake, I tossed and turned in bed—beefcake, gamecock, himbo, beefcake—thinking of my brilliant future as an auctioneer, thinking of my future teeth.

My perseverance, discretion, and discipline during Master Oklahoma's course earned me a grant for a six-month advanced course at the Missouri Auction School in the

United States. The New Jersey grant, the most coveted, was won by Mr. Morato, he of the scissors. I don't bear him any ill will; he probably deserved it. The course in Missouri wasn't up to my expectations, because it focused on the sale of cattle. But it was worth the effort, as I came back from the United States speaking good English. It was also during my time in Missouri that I conceived and developed the theory of my allegoric method. This method is, of course, the product of my own genius, but I was inspired by the daily sermons of our grandmaster auctioneer and country singer, Leroy Van Dyke. Just saying that name, I get the urge to stand up and applaud. I completely disagree with my second-uncle Juan Sánchez Baudrillard when he says that "Americans may have no identity, but they do have wonderful teeth." Van Dyke had both a robust identity *and* good teeth.

Grandmaster Van Dyke had composed the anthem of our guild, "The Auctioneer," which recounts the story of a boy from Arkansas who wants to learn to be an auctioneer and starts to practice every day in the barn of the farm where he lives, with the animals as his audience. When his father and mother realize that he has talent, they send him to auction school, where he grows to become a full-fledged auctioneer.

Listening to Leroy Van Dyke sing "The Auctioneer"—which is also the central theme of my favorite film, *What Am I Bid?*—gave me the impetus I needed to fine-tune the conceptual details of my allegoric method. I'd realized that there was a gap in my profession—a gap that I had to fill. There was not a single auctioneer, adept though he might be in the frantic calling of numbers, or expert in the manipulation of the commercial and emotional value of the lots, who was able to say anything worth hearing about his objects, because he didn't understand or wasn't interested in them as such, only in their exchange value. I finally saw the meaning of the words Master Oklahoma had once spoken with an air of resigned sadness: "We auctioneers are mere hired heralds between the paradise and hell of supply and demand." I, however, was going to reform the art of auctioneering. I would bury the word *herald* in the distant past of my profession with my new method. I wasn't just a lowly seller of objects but, first and foremost, a lover and collector of good stories, which is the only honest way of modifying the value of an object. End of declaration.

I returned from the United States brimming with ambition and ready to forge a path toward my new teeth. The first thing I did was to organize a private auction. I sold one or two pieces of Flaca's furniture and, with the proceeds, was able to buy new pieces for myself and pay six months rent on an apartment. I never saw Flaca again, thank God. But neither did I see Siddhartha for many years. Always, there was something dying inside my chest.

I focused on my profession. I began by auctioning furniture in the Portales neighborhood. Afterward, I met Angelica. I auctioned cars in Cuernavaca. I met Erica. I started traveling more and more. On those trips, I began to gather a collection of objects that I bought at very reasonable prices at special sales. I auctioned antiques across Europe;

real estate in California; memorabilia in São Paulo. I went on auctioning. I met Esther—and so on and so forth until the prostate kicked in, and then I stopped counting women, but not auctions. I auctioned jewels, houses, ancient art, contemporary art, wine, cattle, libraries, and vast assets impounded from the drug trade. I lined my pockets swindling millionaires with a tap of the gavel: going, going, gone.

But I'm no arriviste. I guess I could have owned ten apartments in Miami, but instead I decided to buy land back in my childhood neighborhood, in Ecatepec. With this in mind, I purchased two plots, side by side, in the lovely Calle Disneylandia: it's important to invest in national assets. Added together, I think the two plots were several hectares in size, though I've never bothered to do the math, as I'm not tightfisted either. On one of the plots, I erected a colorful three-story house with towers, being careful to leave enough rebar in place for further development, and not to evade taxes, as most people do in Mexico. On the adjoining lot, I built a warehouse in which I stored all the objects I'd collected during my life. Opposite this, I built my auction house. One day, I was going to construct a suspension bridge to connect the two buildings. I'd already drawn up the plans. Then, in honor of my grandmasters, I was going to inaugurate it officially as the Oklahoma-Van Dyke Auction House. All that was lacking was the land-use permit from the local council, which will always be granted—mañana.

It would be inelegant of me to finish my story by listing the benefits my arduous training and natural talent for auctioneering brought to both me and my community. I only wish to set down biography-wise that, in the year 2000, during a weekend trip to Miami, where I went to auction automobiles, the long struggle against the ignominy in which I was born and grew up finally came to an end. On a Sunday evening, after receiving a hefty check for having advantageously auctioned thirty-seven pickup trucks, I went with some colleagues to an auction of contraband memorabilia in a karaoke bar in Little Havana. They had met some apparently lovely lady friends the night before and had arranged to join them there. They promised it would be worth the effort. It's not my habit to indulge in licentious behavior or do business on Sundays, but I decided to accompany them. It was to my great peace of mind that the four ladies, when they appeared, looked rather the worse for wear anyway.

When the auction began, I thought that there would be nothing to tempt me, since the memorabilia on offer was clearly also fifth rate: a watch belonging to some U.S. politician or other, cigars belonging to who-knows-what Cuban millionaire, a letter written by some unknown hirsute novelist who had traveled to the island in the 1930s. I had no intention of blowing my check, but, without the least warning, the god of tiny details set paradise before me. And paradise doesn't come cheap. Right there, in the depths of the Sunday solitude of a Little Havana auction, I found them: my new teeth.

In the small glass box the auctioneer held high lay waiting for me the sacred teeth of none other than Marilyn Monroe. Yes indeed, the teeth of the Hollywood diva. They were perhaps slightly yellowed, I believe because divas tend to smoke. There was a feeling of tension and unease in the air when the auctioneer opened the bidding. Several ladies who had seen better days, including one of our lady friends, already had their eyes on them. A fat man in outdated clothes spread a wad of bills on his bar table and stood up to light a cigar, to intimidate us I think. But I dug in my heels and got them: the teeth—my teeth—went to me.

I showed such skill in the bidding that one of the lady friends—the worst of the four, a journalist with hair stiff like a doormat from too much dying, and sagging cheeks—wrote an article about the auction that appeared in the *Miami Sun*. Clearly jealous of my achievement, because she too wanted the teeth, her report was stark and twisted. What did I care? She'll soon be eating her words, I thought, while I'll be dining with my Marilyn Monroe teeth. As soon as I got back to Mexico, each of the teeth belonging to the Venus of the big screen was transplanted into my mouth by a world-class dental surgeon, the renowned Dr. Luis Felipe Fabre, owner of Il Miglior Fabbro, the best cosmetic dental clinic and depository in Mexico City. I did save ten of my old teeth, the best-looking ones, for later, just in case.

For months after the operation, I couldn't keep the grin off my face. I showed everyone the infinite line of my new smile, and whenever I passed a mirror or a shop window that reflected my image, I would raise my hat in a gentlemanly fashion and smile at myself. My thin, ungainly body and my rather ungrounded life had acquired serious aplomb with the appearance of my new teeth. My luck was without equal, my life was a poem, and I was certain that one day, someone was going to write the beautiful tale of my dental autobiography. End of story.

℘ 在一個人的頭上的每一個齒比鑽石更有價值。

[Each tooth in the head of a man
is worth more than a diamond.]

BOOK II

The Hyperbolics

The regular connection between a sign, its sense, and its reference is of such a kind that to the sign there corresponds a definite sense and to that in turn a definite reference, while to a given reference (an object) there does not belong only a single sign.

—GOTTLOB FREGE

B Y THE YEAR 2011, MEXICANS HAD LOST THEIR MINDS. Everybody was at war with everybody else, and there was a general climate of antagonism and bitterness—a sense of living on the verge of calamity. It had been some time since I'd been summoned to call an auction. I believe this was because Mexicans are also like crabs in a bucket, and this needs no further explanation. My skills languished, unused. I had also stopped traveling, principally because I'd realized that despite the Mexicans, who make every possible effort to ruin everything, Mexico is glorious. In my opinion, outside my native land, only Paris is worth a mention, but even so, we all know that the city of Campeche beats Paris hands down. End of comment.

Rather than frittering away my money on trips, I'd spent the subsequent years in my own neighborhood, collecting the stories and objects that chance threw in my path or that I found in the local junkyard—a beautiful establishment whose owner, my friend Jorge Ibargüengoitia, gave me special access to for being a loyal client. Between what I'd acquired on my international travels and my new local collections, I had amassed an admirable estate. I knew that one day I'd hold a grand auction in my own house, in which I would offer my treasures to people worthy of the privilege; refined people, people of great breadth of vision. But all that was still in the future, and I am a patient man. The suspension bridge connecting the warehouse to the auction house still had to be finished, the land-use permit had to be obtained, comfortable chairs for the bidders bought, and, most importantly, I had to employ someone to put together my catalog of collectibles.

For the lucky man, even the cock lays an egg, as Napoleón sings. One summer day, Father Luigi Amara, parish priest of Saint Apolonia's, came to offer me his help. Or so I thought. He explained that his church had gone into economic recession as a collateral effect of the global crisis. He was in need of my services as an auctioneer and proposed a project that, he promised, would benefit me too—both in spiritual and material terms. And why lie? The economic crisis had affected me as well. I needed the money that Father Luigi assured me we would make if we joined forces in organizing an auction of collectibles in his church.

Father Luigi's plan was simple. Once a month, Saint Apolonia's offered a service for residents of the neighborhood care home for the elderly, called Serene Twilight, or maybe Sweet Twilight, or perhaps just Twilight—some name like that, as depressing as it was predictable. The monthly mass for these old people was to be held the following Sunday. The majority of them, according to Father Luigi, were from wealthy families. Advanced in years, but solvent, he said. We had to take maximum advantage of the venue and context of the mass to get some money out of them. We would sell that senile but well-heeled congregation a selection of my collectibles in order to raise funds for the parish: 30 percent for me; 70 percent for the church.

At first I thought the balance was unfair, considering that Father Luigi's contribution was restricted to the use of his church and—at only the most distant remove—the bidders, who, numerous though they might be, were still just sickly old dodderers. With such an audience, the chances of a good auction were close to zero. But the reverend father cautioned me to think of the poor souls who would be cheered by my presence, and of the salvation of my own good soul. Although I'm not sure I believe in Hell, I do count myself among those who think it's better to be safe than sorry. What's more, Father Luigi readily agreed to my holding a hyperbolic auction, which was most ad hoc to the circumstances.

Of course, Highway, he said. The hyperbole is an effective means of transmission of the great power of the Holy Spirit.

I explained that what I meant was that I could tell stories whose degree of deviation from the value of the conic section of their related objects was greater than zero. In other words, as the great Quintilian had once said, by means of my hyberbolics, I could restore an object's value through "an elegant surpassing of the truth." This meant that the stories I would tell about the lots would all be based on facts that were, occasionally, exaggerated or, to put it another way, better *illuminated*. But Father Luigi, like all those of his profession, often turns a deaf ear to anything you say that doesn't correspond to what he thinks you should have said.

I spent a few days deciding on the best collection to auction to an audience of elderly bidders. I walked around my warehouse, made notes, and, of course, consulted my Gaius Suetonius Tranquillus tome, for inspiration. During those same days—serendipity, luck—I read an article about an auction in which a molar previously belonging to John Lennon had been sold. Lennon's housekeeper, a certain Dot Jarlett, had held on to it for over half a century and had finally sold it to Omega Auction House. Although Omega listed it under an estimated price of sixteen thousand dollars, the piece had gone for thirty-two thousand. A stroke of genius is nothing more than putting A and B together: I remembered that among my collectibles were my old teeth. I am not a naïve man, and I knew that my teeth were not as valuable as John Lennon's, but I could raise their value by the apposite use of my hyperbolic method. For each tooth, I would tell the hypertrue story of one of my favorite people, in the style of the profiles Suetonius wrote. After all, as Quintilian says, a hyperbolic is simply "a fissure in the relationship between style and reality."

I offered my collection and explained my plan to Father Luigi. He agreed, without showing much interest either in my teeth's fascinating details or in the story of John Lennon's molar. That's politicians for you, clergy included: their heads are so full of themselves that they aren't the least bit curious about other people's lives.

I had a final moment of doubt and reluctance before closing the deal. It wouldn't be easy for me to publicly exhibit such an intimate branch of my collection. Moreover, I'd have preferred to save the items for when I held my grand auction. I finally agreed, of course, because I'm not a mean-spirited sort. But also because I remembered a resplendent evening when I'd read about an auction in which, after the death of the Emperor Pertinax in 193, a praetorian guard had sold off the entire Roman Empire. In the light of history, it would have shown a lack of decorum and gravitas on my part not to accept the minor challenge fate had set before me. End of declaration.

The day before the sale, a messenger took the collection of teeth to the church, where my pieces were to spend the night. Early the following morning, Father Luigi came by to pick me up. I was feeling unhinged and shaky from lack of sleep. I had been awake all night with insomnia, probably because there had been a full moon. I suppose Father Luigi interpreted my appearance as a sign of anxiety related to the imminent auction.

Nervous? he asked as we were walking out the monumental gateway into the street.

Not the least, I replied, my hands trembling like a pair of maracas.

We walked on in a silence so difficult to interpret that I preferred not to break it. Halfway there we felt hungry, so we stopped for a strawberry atole at Magalita's stall and continued on our way, sipping from our Styrofoam cups. Once we were standing outside the church, Father Luigi—the

tips of his mustache stained pink with strawberry atole—
returned to the same topic:

You're not going to back out on me now, are you?

Appearances can be deceptive, Father; I'm a stalwart man.

Look, Highway, it isn't going to be easy, but just keep
in mind that the parish has to be saved from the rampant
capitalism that's threatening it. Right? And while you're at
it, you'll be cleansing your soul. Understood?

Understood, Father. But why keep harping on about it?

I'm not harping on. I just want to make it clear that
these people are coming to see you, and their expectations
are high. Maybe you don't realize it, because you live there
inside your ivory tower, but for a lot of people, you're a legend. Everyone around here knows you.

You flatter me, Father. Go on, go on, don't hold back.

But you have to take into account, Highway, that there
are people who don't necessarily love you very much. They
all know you, and some admire you, but others don't like
you one little bit; some perhaps hate you.

I thought I caught a whiff of sweetening the pill. Well,
like who?

Like your son.

Siddhartha's coming?

Of course.

But you told me it would be just old rich people turning up to buy the teeth. That's what we agreed on.

Yes, but when Siddhartha heard that you'd be selling
part of your legendary collection, he wanted to see you in
action. He's curious about you.

Bring on the violins!

I was afraid you'd say something like that.

What do you expect? I'm a serious auctioneer. Not just someone's clown.

Don't get riled, no one's saying you are. Just remember that this church is in crisis.

As you already mentioned.

So, are you ready, Highway?

I'm almost going cold, Father.

That's good.

Just one other thing, Father. Do you know the story of Little Red Riding Hood in reverse?

Sorry?

I always say it through before auctions: it loosens my tongue and oils my jaw. Perhaps you'd like to say it with me.

How does it go?

Ttleli Red Dingri Hood was walking through the restfo, la-la-tra, la-la-tra, when suddenly, a big ryhai wolf appeared.

Very good, Highway, very good. You keep at it, and at ten fifteen, go into the church through the sacristy door. I'll be giving the final blessing. Mass finishes at ten thirty. In the sacristy, you'll find an altar boy who'll give you a contract to sign; a mere formality. Then he'll show you to the pulpit from which you'll conduct the auction. O.K.?

Kayo, Father.

Fine.

Listen, Father. Is he a good kid?

Who? Siddhartha? He's a hard worker.

What does he do?

He's something of a guard, like you were. He works as an art curator in the gallery next to the juice factory, not in the factory itself.

Well I never! My father always said that genetics is a science full of gods.

Anyway, it's getting late and I have to go inside to put on my vestments. Are we all set?

Can I just say one last thing, Father?

Yes, go ahead.

With all due respect, and no mockery intended, you've got a bit of pink in your mustache.

Father Luigi disappeared under the arch of the doorway, tugging at his mustache and beard with a hand wrapped in the end of his cassock. Until the stroke of ten fifteen, I went on reciting the inverted Little Red Riding Hood story to myself, walking round and round the almost deserted square in front of the church: Where are you going dayto Ttleli Red Dingri Hood? To my thermogrand's house in the restfo.

Among the parishioners entering through the door in small groups, I suddenly made out Siddhartha's face: the little sprout was the spitting image of me. I hadn't seen him since I'd left Flaca, because that filthy sow had forbidden it. But it can't be said that I didn't do my duty: I sent a check for the child's maintenance every month, until I calculated eighteen years and then I stopped—there's no point in raising scroungers.

Following him out of the corner of my eye, I saw Siddhartha enter the church and began to feel an anxiety attack coming on. A cold sweat in the palm of my hands, trembling in my groin and buttocks, the urge to pee, and the desire to turn tail and run. Was it possible that the presence of my own son could throw me off track in this way? I sat on the edge of a raised flowerbed and conjured up the images of my teachers, Carlos Kenta Yushimito and the peerless Leroy Van Dyke. I'm a man of pedigree, I said to myself, taking deep breaths. I'm a man of greedipe, I repeated aloud. I'm the peerless Highway. Wayhigh! I'm the best auctioneer in the world, I haven't been a bad father, I can imitate Janis Joplin after the second round, I can stand an egg upright, like Columbus, and I can float on my back. Oklahoma had auctioned a pair of scissors; and the praetorian guard, Rome. I too, being obviously a man of that same exalted stripe, could auction my precious teeth. Ichi, ni, san, shi, go, roku, shichi, hachi, and then the big, ryhai wolf took the testshor path through the restfo to the thermogrand's house . . . and he gobbled her up!

In the sacristy, a tall, thin, altar boy was waiting for me and identified himself as Emiliano Monge. He handed me a contract that I had to sign and initial. Ignoring the intricate wording, I signed the pages of the contract one by one and then sat playing helicopters with the pen until the altar boy reappeared in the doorway and beckoned me.

The church was packed to the rafters, and I was struck by the strong scent of talcum in the air; I guess the very elderly, like the very young, use talcum. As I came out of the sacristy and made my way to the pulpit, I put my right hand to my eyes and took in the hall in one long sweep, but I couldn't identify Siddhartha among the rapt crowd. I was by then somewhat eager to see him, to have him see me, to impress him. Behind the pulpit, to which I hesitatingly ascended, my collection of teeth was lined up on a long metal table. I turned my back on them with a sense of sadness. Father Luigi came up and, putting an arm around my shoulders, whispered in my ear, like a football coach, Show 'em what you're worth, hotshot!

I took a deep breath and began: Dear parishioners of Saint Apolonia's, on this day our congregation needs your generosity, will, and commitment. But the words came out in a tone that sounded like a politician past his prime. I tried to modulate my voice, to infuse some enthusiasm into it, offering my audience a broad, toothy smile. We have here before us today pieces of great value, since each contains a story replete with small lessons. Taken together, these stories remind us of the true meaning of one of the most important pieces of wisdom in the Scriptures: "An eye for an eye and a tooth for a tooth." This famous dictum is not a call to vengeance, as is commonly believed, but an invitation to value the small details of objects. God is in the details of teeth. I paused for applause. But the audience merely regarded me with the silent skepticism of cattle.

I managed to keep my focus and continued, raising my voice a little: All the original owners of these teeth were considered social parasites, ne'er-do-wells, and sluggards;

many suffered from dementia, megalomania, graphomania, melancholy, erotomania, and acute egomania. But despite all those negative characteristics, they were the possessors of profound souls and magnificent teeth. In other words, as my uncle Miguel Sánchez Foucault said in relation to something else, these men and women are "singular lives transformed into strange poems through who knows what twists of fate." Taken as a collection, the teeth of these infamous people are, to use an auctioneering term, a "metonymic relic." And you don't have to be superstitious to know that, when used correctly, certain objects can transfer their powerful qualities to us.

I had to restrain myself so as not to overdo it because, as Quintilian suggests, when using hyperbole, "some moderation must be observed, for though every hyperbole is beyond belief, it ought not to be extravagant, since in no other way do writers more readily fall into κακοζηλία, or exorbitant affectation."

I am going to recount for you the fascinating stories of all these teeth, and I would urge you to buy them, take them to your homes, use them, or simply cherish them for persecula seculorum. That is, for forever. Otherwise, I continued, slightly overstating the case in a menacing tone, if these relics don't find owners by the end of this session, they will be sold abroad. And the last thing we need is for the little we have to be carried off by others.

I noted that this latter argument, although it wasn't completely valid, had begun to capture the Cardenist, socialist, national-reconstructive hearts of my audience.

Without further ado, I gave a half turn, moved toward my dental collectibles, picked up the first lot, and, holding it high as I walked back to the pulpit, like a priestess in full Delphic trance, I began my chant with the skill and charm of which only the greatest of my stripe are capable.

HYPERBOLIC LOT NO. 1

Our first lot is a piece in a somewhat deteriorated state. Yet, considering its antiquity, the overall condition is good; one might even say excellent. Significant flattening of the point leads to the supposition that the original owner, Mr. Plato, talked and ate continuously. He was five feet five inches tall and thirty-three and a half inches broad; he was of medium height but robust, with a fighter's build. He had a long, cotton-woolly beard, light brown in color; thick hair of the same hue and texture. Mr. Plato flaunted the conventional fashions of the day and wore his toga loose, without a belt. Neither did he wear sandals.

Mr. Plato once made a comparison between the period of dentition and a man falling in love: "In this state, the soul enters into effervescence and irritation; and this soul, whose wings are just beginning to develop, can be compared to a child whose gums are inflamed and enervated by its first teeth." Lovely, don't you think?

I paused momentarily for greater effect. Wafts of cool morning air were beginning to enter the church through the high main door. I had the sense that a ray of light was falling from the sky, miraculously illuminating the pulpit. I raised my eyes and immediately noticed the altar boy

Monge up in one of the galleries, throwing a spotlight onto me. It wasn't divine light, but even so, it filled me with motivation. I took a breath: Ladies and gentlemen, who will open the bidding for the cavernous tooth of our first infamous man?

A hand was timidly raised at the back of the church: 1,000 pesos. It was followed by another, more eager hand: 1,500. And another, and another, and another. The lot went for 5,000 pesos. Not at all bad, for a warm-up. It was bought by a small, elderly, opulently dressed woman. Quintilian explains that "there is in all men a natural propensity to magnify or extenuate what comes before them, and no one is contented with the exact truth." I believe that's why the most worn-out tooth in my collection went for such a high price. I cleared my throat and continued with my infamy.

HYPERBOLIC LOT NO. 2

The owner of this tooth, of North African origin, was of medium height, with spindly arms and smooth skin. There is some argument as to whether he was black or white. In my opinion, he was unambiguously black. His name was Augustine of Hippo, and on the top of his head was a bald patch bearing some resemblance to the mouth of a volcano. Had we been capable of looking into the bowels of that volcano, we would have discovered one of the most labyrinthine memories ever spawned by the union of Mother Nature and God the Father. That prodigious memory, the inferior hatchway of which was this very tooth we have before us today, was once compared by

Mr. Augustine himself to an infinite stretch of open countryside, where all the copies of the impressions entering through the senses were stored, in addition to their many variations; there were all the things that had been entrusted to it; the abstract numbers of mathematics; his own earliest memories, both accurate and false; and even, in its furthest reaches, the things that seemed to be forgotten but, in fact, were not.

Do you see this hole on the crown of the piece? If we had been able to enter through that orifice and move upward through the labyrinth of channels that connect the mouth with the cranium in which the teeth nestle, in one of the most remote chambers of the brain we would find this memory: a young student of rhetoric—who is, of course, Augustine himself—is suffering the mortifying pain of a dreadful toothache. The young man is surrounded by family and friends, all of whom believe he will soon be dead since his pain is so severe that he cannot open his mouth to communicate his affliction. At a given moment, he gathers his strength and writes on a wax tablet: Pray for my health. The friends and family pray and the young lad is cured. A miracle. He then decides to dedicate his life to God by means of a book that he begins to write just a few years later, his famous *Confessions*. That's right, this gentleman wrote the great *Confessions* because of a toothache. Who will open the bidding for the memorious tooth of Augustine of Hippo?

Several parishioners showed interest. The first offered five hundred. The next wanted to offer less rather than more, appealing to my compassion by alleging a recently diagnosed dementia. But his companions on the pew quickly silenced him and forced him to sit down, arguing that his case was nothing special. At the end of the round of bidding, Saint Augustine's tooth was bought by a lady poet with the face and body of an owl for three thousand pesos. I took the third piece from the table behind me and returned to the pulpit.

HYPERBOLIC LOT NO. 3

The owner of this lot was an eminent man of harmonious proportions, with a notoriously beautiful face. He was christened Francesco Petracco, but went by the name of Petrarch, I believe because it sounded more patriarchal. He was a poet and songwriter. Slothful, as they all are; fickle and mellifluous, but skillful.

Some years ago, a group of scientists opened his tomb because the honorable Italian government wished to have an exact, definitive copy of his face made to commemorate the seven hundredth anniversary of his death. On reassembling the cranium, the scientists suspected that the bones very probably belonged to a woman. They had DNA tests done both on the ribs and an incisor. Several days later, Dr. Carameli, leader of the team, made a public declaration stating that the tests had confirmed their suspicions: the head was "apocryphal." The loss of the original head was blamed on a certain Father Tomasso Martinelli, a poor, seventeenth-century priest who, in addition, was judged to be an alcoholic. Without further evidence, Martinelli was pronounced guilty of having sold Petrarch's beautiful head to some punters in order to buy a few casks of wine. What didn't occur to any Italian politician was that it was perhaps the corpse in the tomb that belonged to someone else, and that the head was Mr. Petrarch's.

I can assure you that this is one of Petrarch's teeth. One irrefutable proof is the fact that it is an exact reflection of his character. The teeth are the true windows to the soul; they are the tabula rasa on which all our vices and all our virtues are inscribed. Mr. Petrarch had a choleric nature, keen intelligence, and a weakness for sensual pleasures: he was hornier than a goat, and it's easy to tell by just one look at the length of this incisor. It's said that Petracco was once found at the doors of the church of Saint Clara, ogling the widowed, single, and married women who entered there to commend their souls to Our Lady of Saint Clara at all hours of the day. The gentleman was a veritable rake. He would make flirtatious comments, sing ribald lyrics of his own composition, leer at their ankles and necks. For years he plagued the wife of the prominent Count Hugues de Sade, the beautiful and discreet Laura de Noves. Naturally, he never gained the attention of the demure lady.

It is also known that this infamous man was in the habit of writing intimate letters to people who were, quite clearly, imaginary and, what's worse, by anyone's reckoning, dead. Mr. Petrarch termed the products of this demoniacal practice "familiar letters" and sometimes "senile letters." To my mind, "senile" would be more appropriate than "familiar." Senile or, I'd say, without wishing to offend those present, "demented": he wrote demented letters to the dead. Petrarch collected all the letters he wrote. In total, he managed to compile 128 senile and 350 familiar letters. He was a daring collector, an idiotically annoying slacker—and brilliant. The depths of his infamy and genius are without equal, so in this case I'm obliged to set the reserve price high. Who will give me a 1,500 bid?

An almost totally bald man, with a scrawny neck and a chubby collection-box face raised the bidding by 100. I noticed when he opened his mouth to call out the amount that it didn't contain a single tooth. No one else raised a hand. My incisor went for 1,600. Father Luigi, standing like a Cerberus by my line of collectibles, passed the fourth piece to me. He raised an eyebrow, encouraging me to continue.

HYPERBOLIC LOT NO. 4

This lot has, for many years, been one of the most sought after in the market for portable oral collectibles. Its owner was a short man, broad in the beam, with a snub nose and a forehead like a pig's backside. Megalomania had no limits in the soul of this infamous man of minute stature. On more than one occasion, he said, "I study myself more than any other subject; I am my physics and my metaphysics." He was scarcely four feet ten inches tall. His hair was sparse and straggly, but his ideas were prolific and forceful.

Mr. Montaigne, the original owner of this tooth, had a serene, honest gaze. His face had an expression somewhere between melancholic and jovial. His ineptitude in everyday activities, however, reached the point of burlesque: the handwriting in his manuscripts was illegible; he was incapable of folding a letter properly; he couldn't saddle a horse or carry a hawk and fly her; he had no authority at all over dogs; nor could he communicate with horses. A waste of space, it would seem. A waste of space, nonetheless, who enjoyed good oral health, with the exception of recurrent tonsillitis. He preferred his flesh almost raw, including fish. He didn't like any fruit or vegetable, other than melons. That is perhaps the reason why the tooth is in such good condition. Moreover, the quality is sublime: it is fine, slender, slightly pointed. The secret of his long-lived teeth? Mr. Montaigne was given to saying: "J'ay aprins dés l'enfance à les froter de ma serviette, et le matin, et à l'entrée et issue de la table." That is to say, from childhood he learned to rub them with a napkin every morning, and both before and after dinner. Who will open the bidding for Montaigne's ultraclean tooth?

A sudden wave of enthusiasm welled up among the bidders. I sold my favorite lot for six thousand pesos. It was bought by an old woman with a forgettable face and a Mediterranean build—it's a mystery why all female Mediterranean bodies look like eggplants after the age of fifty.

By the end of that round of bidding, I was beginning to feel like John Paul II. I imagined myself entering a packed stadium, greeting the vast crowd, hand raised high. I'd have been the envy of Mussolini, the envy of Madonna, Sting, Bono, Lennon, and Leroy Van Dyke himself. I finally caught sight of Siddhartha—he was sitting on a pew toward the back of the church. Emboldened, I began the next lot without a pause.

HYPERBOLIC LOT NO. 5

Only one of Mr. Rousseau's teeth remains in existence, but what a tooth! This adorable, infamous man had aristocratic features in which the slightest trace of facial expression was stifled by a vigilant, tyrannical conscience.

His eyes were expressive and mobile, but his gaze was not commanding. Despite his undeniable intelligence, his sense of humor was infantile. He fervently believed in man's kindly nature, especially his own. This gentleman wore shoulder pads, as he was rather lacking in that part of his anatomy. This deficit, however, was compensated by a manly jaw—broad, square, with a slight cleft in the center—within which lay the teeth forever invisible to the world. They were so ugly that he never showed them, not even in private. He himself was conscious of the awful monstrosity of his teeth. He was an avid reader of Plutarch, from which he learned some virtues and many vices. In *Parallel Lives,* Plutarch writes that the courtesan Flora never left her lover without ensuring that she bore on her lips the marks of his teeth. After reading that, Jean-Jacques also acquired the habit of asking his lovers to bite him before leaving. But he didn't once return the bite, since, as he said, his teeth were "épouvantables"; that is, horrifying. He wasn't exaggerating.

The fact that only one piece of Rousseau's has been preserved is not due to his hygienic practices, which were those of a decent man, but to his bad luck. Mr. Rousseau spent a good part of his life walking. The good-for-nothing rambler walked as if the welfare of mankind depended on his steps. One day, he went out for a stroll and was knocked over by a dog. Apparently, the animal approached him at great speed and got tangled up in his legs for an instant; our infamous man went flying toward the ditch bordering the road and lost an item, possibly the very one that we have here today. It is so horrible that it deserves a monument. This piece, in particular, is like a spiral staircase to a skylight once covered in plaque. Who will open the bidding for this solitary, furry tooth of Rousseau?

People are morbid and sordid, even when they don't mean to be. I believe that it was only in order to be able to inspect the battered tooth that the bidders offered more than ever. After a heated round of bidding, the tooth was bought by a man with a foreign accent, a complete set of teeth, but a cryptic smile, for 7,500 pesos.

HYPERBOLIC LOT NO. 6

> There has never been a man with such a protruding lower jaw than Mr. Charles Lamb, who suffered from such a severe prognathous that he had to keep his lips slightly parted all the time. If he didn't, one of his canine teeth rubbed against his tongue and upper lip, causing a collection of extremely painful sores and ulcers. It would not be unreasonable to imagine that everything Mr. Lamb wrote—which was a lot and very good—was the product of the tortuous disposition of his teeth. He had a schoolboy stammer, and his writing was equally stuttering. He once wrote a stuttering letter to his friend Wordsworth, saying, "I have just now a jagged end of a tooth pricking against my tongue, which meets it half way, in a wantonness of provocation; and there they go at it, the tongue pricking itself, like the viper against the file, and the tooth galling all the gum inside and out to torture; tongue and tooth, tooth and tongue, hard at it; and I to pay the reckoning, till all my mouth is as hot as brimstone."
>
> Eight hundred pesos for Lamb's stuttering tooth! Who will open the bidding? Who will give me more?

Not a single hand was raised, so I continued with the next lot.

We have before us here the tooth of the greatest of the ne'er-do-well sluggards, Mr. G. K. Chesterton: 5 feet 11 inches tall, 310 pounds. He was as broad as the barrels in which cheap wine is aged. The flesh at the nape of his neck hung over his collar, his cheeks were bulging, and his eyes hooded from an almost perpetual frown. He drank astonishing quantities of milk.

The tooth may be in a lamentable condition, but it is a truly charismatic one. It is thought that the damage to this tooth was caused by Mr. Chesterton's self-confessed inclination for chewing marbles. I quote from memory: "We talk rightly of giving stones for bread: but there are in the Geological Museum certain rich crimson marbles, certain split stones of blue and green, that make me wish my teeth were stronger."

There is one story about this gentleman that I like particularly. He left his house one day, possibly chewing a marble, with the single, firm intention of drawing with chalk on a sheet of brown paper. He put six very brightly colored sticks of chalk in his pockets, slipped a few sheets of brown paper under his arm, and went out—hat, stick, and jacket—to depict the world around him. At a given moment, when the hippopotamic idler had reached the gentle countryside of the downs, he was approached by a domestic cow—incidentally, the second-most imbecilic member of the animal kingdom, the first being, obviously, the giraffe, and the third the Australian kangaroo.

Mr. Chesterton made a couple of dispassionate attempts to sketch the cow in chalk, but he soon noticed that his talent came to an end where the hind legs of the quadruped began. After weighing the matter up for a moment, he resolved to draw, clenching the piece of chalk between his teeth, the soul of the mammal instead of its external appearance. He depicted it in purple with silver highlights. End of story. Who will open the bidding?

There was a long silence.

Who will open the bidding? I repeated.

The tooth of the ne'er-do-well layabout went for only 2,500 pesos.

HYPERBOLIC LOT NO. 8

Some teeth are tormented. Such is the case of this one, the property of Mrs. Virginia Woolf. When she was just thirty years old, a psychiatrist posited the theory that her emotional ills were due to an excess of bacteria around the roots of her teeth. He decided to extract the three most seriously affected ones. Nothing changed. During the course of her life, several more teeth were extracted, but it made no difference. None at all, rien de rien. Mrs. Woolf died by her own hand, with many false teeth in her oral cavity. Her acquaintances only ever saw her smile at her funeral. It's said that, lying dead in her half-open coffin in the center of the living room, her lips were spread in a smile that lit up her sharp, intelligent features. Who will offer 8,000 pesos for this tortured tooth? Anyone?

After a heavy silence, an elderly man, with a stubborn but respectable face, bought it for 8,900 pesos. As soon as I had called the final "gone," letting the head of my gavel fall onto the inclined surface of the pulpit, I heard the squawking of a bird among the congregation.

Shut up, Jacinto, someone immediately yelled.

But the squawk repeated. I then noticed that a small man in the third row was standing on one of the pews. Taking off his hat, he looked at me from some distant interior place and slowly opened his mouth to utter another squawk. An indistinguishable murmur crackled from the mass of the audience.

Shut up and sit down, Jacinto, said the voice again.

A number of others seconded the command. But the gentleman ignored the attempts of his fellow pensioners to stop him, and I, with the authority conferred on me by the pulpit, ordered them to let him finish. He squawked again, this time more loudly and with greater aplomb. The murmuring died down. Then, with the grace of a professional ballet dancer, the man raised his arms to shoulder level and, without ceasing to squawk, began to slowly flap them. I'm not one of those people who cry easily, but a lump of sadness stuck in my throat. There was something sad and beautiful in the simulated flight of this elderly parishioner.

When the gentleman had finished, he sat down again in his pew and put his hat back on his head. I found it difficult to pick up the thread of the hyperbolics again. Something in the temporal suspension produced by the impossible flight of that old man in the pew of the parish church had touched me.

HYPERBOLIC LOT NO. 9

Our penultimate lot, ladies and gentlemen, exudes an air of mystical melancholy. The tooth itself is crocodilian, but its aura is almost angelic. Note the curve; it is like a wing in ascent. Its owner, Mr. Jorge Francisco Isidoro Luis Borges, was a man of average height. His short, thin legs supported a torso, which was at once solid and svelte. His head was the size of a small coconut, and he had a slender, flexible neck. He was a pantheist. His eyes used to flit from side to side, useless, impenetrable to sunlight but ready to receive the light of beautiful, good ideas. He spoke slowly, as if searching for adjectives in the darkness. How much will you bid?

To my great disillusion, they offered just 2,500 pesos for Borges's melancholy tooth.

HYPERBOLIC LOT NO. 10

Our final collectible lot, ladies and gentlemen, is a molar. Its owner still walks this earth with the parsimony of a mythological animal and the ungrounded spirit of an eternal phantom. The tooth belonged to Mr. Enrique Vila-Matas, and before it existed, it was written. Let me explain. The aforementioned Mr. Vila-Matas once dreamed that one of his molars fell out while he was asleep and that a man named Raymond Roussel came into the bedroom, woke him up by shouting like a sergeant major, providing him with a series of unreasonable bits of advice related to his eating habits. Before going back out through the door,

Raymond Roussel picked up the tooth lying among the sheets and put it in the pocket of his jacket.

The following morning, Mr. Vila-Matas felt his teeth to check if he had in fact lost one. They were all present and correct. Being a somewhat superstitious man, he then decided to write a story to avoid the possibility of this loss ever happening in real life.

Several years later, while eating king prawns with his friend Sergio Pitol, in the town of Potrero in Veracruz State, Mr. Vila-Matas told Pitol about the episode with the tooth. However, in the middle of his story, a molar did in fact come loose, and fell into his plate of king prawns. Mr. Sergio Pitol, who is a man of great wisdom and mysticism, asked Vila-Matas to give him the molar, as he knew a shaman in the town who buried the teeth of the best men and women, and with them conducted a white magic ritual that guaranteed they would be preserved for sweet eternity in human memory. Mr. Vila-Matas handed it to him with a degree of reluctance, but finally trusting that his friend would keep his word.

That Potrero shaman was my uncle, the illustrious Cadmus Sánchez, son of my paternal great aunt Telefasa Sánchez. When my uncle Cadmus died a few years ago, his son, my cousin, an idiot who deserves no further mention, rang to tell me that his father had left me something in his will and that if I wanted to claim my inheritance, I should come to Potrero at once. I boarded a bus that same night.

My uncle Cadmus, as you will have by now guessed, had left me the collection of infamous teeth that he had buried under a beautiful mango tree on the outskirts of Potrero. In a note, he explained that the ground was going to be expropriated by the government within a few months in order to build a power station. So he charged me with digging up the sacred teeth and seeking a brighter future for them. Here we find ourselves, dear parishioners, and here we find the final tooth of the collection. The respected Mr. Vila-Matas's molar. Who will open the bidding?

The honest truth is that I don't remember how much I got for it. I was at the very peak of the stupor brought on by the almost toxic atmosphere of an, up to that point, successful auction. Auctioning is, for me, a highly addictive activity, just as gambling, certain drugs, sex, or lying is for others. When I was young, I used to come out of public sales with the desire to sell off everything: the cars I saw in the street, the traffic lights, the buildings, the dogs, people, the insects that distractedly crossed my field of vision.

The parishioners were equally intoxicated by the stupefying humors of the auction. They wanted more. It was obvious: they wanted to go on buying. And I like to please people, not out of submissiveness and an excess of deference, but because I'm a considerate, affable sort. For want of more pieces, I decided, in a stroke of genius that can be attributed to the zeal that had taken hold of me, to auction off myself.

I am Gustavo Sánchez Sánchez, I said. I am the peerless Highway. And I am my teeth. They may seem to you to be yellowed and a little worse for wear, but I can assure you: these teeth once belonged to none other than Marilyn Monroe, and she needs no introduction. If you want them, you will have to take me along too. I gave no further explanation.

Who will open the bidding? I asked in a quiet, calm tone, catching Siddhartha's eyes, fixed on me.

Who will open the bidding for me and my teeth? I repeated to an undaunted audience. A hand went up. Exactly what I'd imagined occurred. For the price of 1,000 pesos, Siddhartha bought me.

ℛ 瘋狂的人 誰是永遠反對，花崗岩塊，
完整和不變，過去他的牙齒咬緊

[Demented is the man who is always clenching his teeth on
that solid, immutable block of stone that is the past.]

BOOK III

The Parabolics

Call something a *rigid designator* if in every possible world it designates the same object. . . . Of course, we don't require that the objects exist in all possible worlds. . . . A designator rigidly designates a certain object if it designates that object wherever the object exists.

—SAUL KRIPKE

M Y UNCLE MARCELO SÁNCHEZ-PROUST ONCE WROTE
in his diary:

> When a man is asleep, he has in a circle round him the
> chain of the hours, the sequence of the years, the order of
> the heavenly host. Instinctively, when he awakes, he looks
> to these, and in an instant reads off his own position on
> the earth's surface and the time that has elapsed during
> his slumbers, but this ordered procession is apt to grow
> confused, and to break its ranks.

I never feel confused or break anything when I wake up.
I'm unbreakable and unconfoundable, like all simple men.
Every day, I return to the waking world with the beautiful, uncomplicated certainty of my modest but firm early-morning erections.

And I'm not unusual. Quite the reverse. Recent scientific studies show that the very first thing the great majority of men notice on waking up in the morning is the turgidity and rigidity of their sexual organs. There is no mystery in this. During the night, the body pumps blood to the male member to maintain the temperature needed for its health and normal functioning. As a consequence, many men wake up with a powerful, proud erection, the intensity of which also acts as a first anchor to the world during the transition from sleep to wakefulness. Women don't experience anything like that, and so often feel completely disoriented when they open their eyes. They don't have that gentle Charon to mark out the road from one world to the other.

This phenomenon of the male constitution, known in common parlance as "the tent effect," is a biological event, and in no way psychological. But like so many other biological phenomena, it can quickly become a matter of mental and spiritual health. If the erection is left unattended and has to go down on its own—during the first sips of coffee or under the shower—a man accumulates malignant humors that engulf him in resentment and rage throughout the day. He becomes circumspect, taciturn, secretly aggressive, and can even begin to harbor perfidious thoughts toward his fellow citizens, including members of his family and his colleagues. However, if the person who sleeps beside him shows empathy and frees the organ from the accumulation of bodily fluids, the man remains mild and self-controlled the whole day, one might even say easygoing and philanthropic. End of explanation.

My uncle Marcelo Sánchez Proust, who had many theories about many things, used to say that a man should marry a woman who had an understanding attitude toward this natural condition of men. "You have to find a madame," he would say, "who tempers the fury that accumulates during the long sleepless hours of men who are sensitive to the elasticity of time." Whatever that might have meant, he would go on to add that that was why he had married my aunt Nadia and remained faithful to her until death did them part (the poor woman died of angina pectoris, like our founding father Benito Juárez). It may be that Aunt Nadia hid her light under a bushel, and though she might have dressed like a teacher in an orphanage, she was, undoubtedly, a virtuoso of early-morning fornication.

I, in contrast, never had any luck in that department—perhaps because the luck of a lucky man, as is my case, is distributed so that it doesn't quite reach the most recondite corners of human experience. Like the bell curve theory. Flaca did her duty by me until she got pregnant; that is, for approximately two weeks. And after that, zilch. She was always rather lacking in generosity in relation to other people's needs, above all mine. But neither did I find early-morning solace with the other women in my life. Angelica, who was far from ugly, used to wake up with her mouth smelling of chicken, so it was me who refused physical contact. Erica, on the other hand, had a strange resemblance to the ex-president Felipe Calderón while she was sleeping, I think because her face became a little swollen, particularly the lips, nose, and eyebrows. Much as I would have liked to dissipate my pent-up humors inside her, as soon as I saw her there, puffed up and deformed by sleep, identical to the president of those dark years in Mexico, I would be so terrified that I'd get silently out of bed and tiptoe away to make myself a cup of strong cof-fee. And Esther, finally, was extremely bad tempered in the mornings. I never dared to snuggle up to her for fear she'd set about me with the chain she kept handy in her drawer. So I used to let her make the first move, which usually consisted of giving me—chain in hand—a difficult-to-interpret polysyllabic command along the lines of Highway, onyerknees an' givittongue. Or maybe: Highway, muffdivintime. Or simply: Highway, satisfyme. But as—thankfully—Esther almost never made the first move, I learned to resign myself to my fate. I've got an unparalleled talent for resignation, like all Catholic men.

That morning, the morning of my brief captivity after the day of the auction, the first thing I noticed was the erection, whose faithful, shield-bearer presence returned me daily to the consciousness of the world. I tried to ignore it, and fell back to sleep. I don't know how much time passed—sec-onds, perhaps minutes. When I began to regain my senses once again, the first thing I noticed was a pungent smell, like newly varnished wood, and I immediately felt an unbearable burning sensation between my eyes. I was lying on a hard, wooden surface, but was sweating profusely at the temples. My head was throbbing hard and fast, like a bird's tiny heart. I then felt a strange swelling in my tongue, and, at the back of my mouth, the slightly metallic taste of blood. In a silence that only accentuated the irregular palpitations in my chest, I heard a faint purring, perhaps a muffled snore, almost a groan. I figured that I must be in a room where other people were asleep. I preferred not to open my eyes, thinking I'd perhaps been put in an old people's home or a jail, and tried to get back to sleep, without quite succeeding.

The only thing I remembered after the auction in the church was having gone out into the street holding Siddhartha's hand. At that moment, it crossed my mind that the last time I'd held it, his hand had fit inside mine. But I immediately stifled that thought, because it made me want to hug him, and I sensed he wouldn't want to be hugged. We walked across the square, hand in hand, toward a car that was waiting for us on the corner, me trying to explain to Siddhartha how the hilarious inverted Red Riding Hood story worked. Siddhartha looked straight ahead and completely ignored me, the way parents ignore their children when they're trying to explain complicated things to them. And that was all I remembered; everything else was a white effasure.

With my eyes still closed and trying to doze on, I slowly passed the tip of my tongue over the roof of my mouth. At that moment I went to pieces. When I attempted to move my tongue along the crescent of my teeth, as sacred, graceful, and hallowed as Bernini's St. Peter's Colonnade, I found a large, empty space. Nothing. Not a single tooth. Oh, Marilyn! I raised one hand to my mouth and opened my eyes. I sat up and noticed I had been lying on a bench. With the tip of my fingers, I felt my lips, my tongue, my palate, my naked gums. Nothing, not a single tooth. What would the great architect of St. Peter's have done if he'd turned up at the Vatican one day and noticed that the awe-inspiring Doric columns forming a semicircle around the atrium that heralds the even more glorious heights of the monument to Catholicism were simply not there?

I looked around me, surveying the room where I'd been sleeping, and discovered a hell worse than the one that had installed itself inside my mouth. A clown of superhuman dimensions, projected onto a screen, was contemplating me with a vaguely gentle expression. I was overcome by fear, and though the most logical thing would have been to stand up from the bench and make a run for the half-open door of the small room, my modesty stopped me. My stubborn and—given the circumstances—inexplicable erection made it impossible for me to get to my feet. I scanned the room. From the screens on the four walls, four catatonic clowns were looking at me. I became certain I'd lost it, all my popcorn burnt. The other option, that I had perhaps been kidnapped and was being tortured, was much more ominous, given that this is a country where a human life is worth less than a ticket from Mexico City to Acapulco on the miserable Estrella de Oro line.

Straight in front of me was the enlarged image of a clown with his face painted white, a smile drawn in black around the mouth, and an undersized Chaplinesque bowler perched on top of his bald pate. I turned my head to the right. An image of the same exaggerated proportions showed a clown dressed in a brightly colored bodysuit, the greater part of his face painted blood red, and a bush of yellow hair sprouting from the sides of a huge, chunky noggin. The clown to my left wore a white bodysuit and a yellow duck-feather boa; his face was painted pink, and above his natural eyebrows was a spectrum of unnatural ones that ran up his forehead like a flight of differently colored stairs to a predominantly bald scalp. Needless to say, all three had the characteristic, forbidding button nose. I only gave the clown behind me a quick look, but was able to make out a black shoe with a broad sole, and a face painted red and black. Glimpsed out of the corner of my eye, he appeared to be the most sinister of the four, so I turned my head to the clown in front of me—the one with the white face and undersized bowler. Then, to my deep discomposure, this clown blinked.

I waited a few moments, gripping the edge of my bench, to see if he would repeat the action or if it was just that I was disoriented to the point of hallucination. Not only did the clown blink again, but suddenly, without him opening his mouth, a voice sounded from above my head:

Don't you think that most things are so lovely, Fancio-ulle?

I didn't reply, as he evidently couldn't be referring to me. Highway, you're an imbecile, I thought to myself. Speaking aloud, I managed—if weakly—to repeat: Imbecile.

I didn't recognize my own voice. Without the solid frame of my teeth, the words issuing from my mouth were light, burbling puffs of air, the voice of an old man brought low. Then, that voice sounded again—slow, calm, almost cynical. It mimicked what I'd just said:

Im-be-cile.

Who are you? Where are you? I asked in alarm.

Give it up, Fancioulle.

Pardon?

Give up playing the imbecile, Fancioulle.

You're confusing me with someone else. I am Gustavo Sánchez Sánchez, Highway, at your service.

Give it up, you bastard. Just tell me where you've hidden the makeup removal cream.

I don't know what you're talking about, I replied.

I then noticed that the voice was, in fact, coming from a loudspeaker in the ceiling, and that there were three other speakers, one in each corner of the room.

My cream, bloody Fancioulle. My face is cracking up and I want to take my makeup off.

I don't use cream. I'm neither a woman nor a clown, and I don't make myself up.

So you're not a clown? Bloody, toothless, deceitful Fancioulle.

My name is Gustavo Sánchez Sánchez, but people call me Highway, out of affection.

Give it a rest.

And I'm the best auctioneer in the world.

Yeah? And what did you come to auction to us?

Not knowing how to respond, I held my tongue. The clown went on talking. He asked me if I knew the parable of the pearl, and, without waiting for me to reply, he began to give me a detailed explanation. He spoke to me as one does to a small child or a foreigner, pronouncing each word slowly and correctly:

Jesus said, "My Father's kingdom can be compared to a person who had a treasure hidden in his field but did not know it. And when he died he left it to his son. The son did not know about the treasure either. He took over the field and sold it. The buyer ploughed the field, discovered the treasure, and began to lend money at interest to whomever he wished."

Do you understand this, Fancioulle?

Yes, of course. I went to Sunday School.

So what does it mean?

It means you should check what's in your father's field before you sell it.

Imbecile.

The clown blinked and gave a long, unembarrassed yawn. Then he said: You're the most unexciting, stupid person I know, Fancioulle. He immediately closed his eyes and, it seemed to me, from the sound of his breathing, that he had fallen into a deep sleep.

I was certain that I had gone to hell. During the long family meals I had to endure in my childhood, my cousin, Juan Pablo Sánchez Sartre, who used to wear white plastic flip-flops and couldn't hold his drink, would inevitably tell us—around the time when the dessert was being served—that we were hell. He used to shout at us, curse us; sometimes he threw objects or scraps of food left scattered on the tablecloth, especially soft grains of rice, and then left, slamming the door loudly behind him. We wouldn't see him again until the next family gathering, when the same act was repeated, with slight variations. And so it went, every couple of months, until one day Juan Pablo committed suicide by having a heart attack during spinning class under the effects of a powerful amphetamine. End of family memory. But it could be that there was something in poor Juan Pablo's theory. Since then, I've always thought that hell is the people you could one day become. The most frightening ones. For Juan Pablo, they were his most contemptible relations—the corrupt uncles, the aunts smelling of cosmetics, the unremarkable cousins. Other people are afraid of their enemies and superiors; others of the loonies who walk along the streets talking to themselves or the madwomen who scour their skin in public; some can't tolerate the presence of the poor, amputees, vagrants. For me, there's no one more ominous than a human being dressed up as a clown, probably because I've always been scared of being perceived as one. And there I was, toothless, lying on a bench in front of videotaped projections of enormous buffoons, dozing—or maybe depressed to the point of catatonia—being mistaken for one of them.

I felt the urge to run, the erection that had initially held me back no longer being an impediment. But immediately I realized that there was no point in running. Where would I go? And what good would it do? Instead, I stood up and walked around the room. It was a square no larger than twenty paces across and twenty wide. Bare, except for the four large screens upon which the sleeping clowns were projected. Near the door that had been left ajar, a small wall text read: "Ugo Rondinone. *Where do we go from here?* Four video installations, sound, ink on wall, wood, yellow neon light." I pushed the door fully open and peeked out. The room gave onto another, much larger and well illuminated. I crossed the threshold and walked around that larger space. Placed in odd spots and in corners were a series of objects: a billboard featuring a horse inside a hotel room, a sleeping stuffed dog, a couple of plush rat and mouse costumes, a hairy prosthetic leg, a tiny baobab tree, a pile of whistles, a music score on a tripod, and a fake window consisting solely of light thrown onto the wall by halogen spotlights. The last of these I found particularly beautiful, and thought it might be worth collecting, or at least copying the idea for my warehouse, which didn't have as many windows as a decent place should.

I was trying to gauge how much the spotlights weighed when I heard the same phlegmatic voice in the other room. I sauntered back, taking my time.

Are you still here, Fancioulle?

Where am I supposed to go? I said, returning to sit on my bench.

You said you'd fetch my mother's vw from the pound, and don't try to pretend you didn't. It was your fault they towed it away, Fancioulle.

I didn't say I'd do anything. Who are you? Where are you?

Here, on your right.

Now I understood. Although the voice was the same, it was now purportedly coming from the direction of the clown in the brightly colored bodysuit. If it was intended to be convincing, this was a really bad production. The second clown was blaming me for having parked a white vw in a space that was obviously for disabled drivers, and, in addition to showing a lack of concern for invalids on my part, it had been, he claimed, an act of extreme passive-aggressive violence toward him and his progenitor. Generalized lack of consideration for others and passive-aggressive violence were, as he went on to explain, typical characteristics of depression. It was, therefore, clear that I was deeply depressed, so he respectfully suggested that I go to a psychologist or psychoanalyst, and he also advised me to sleep at least eight hours a day, stop drinking alcohol, and definitely take a lot of exercise, since that leads to the production of large amounts of serotonin in the cerebellum and the hypothalamus. I interrupted:

Why don't you go get the vw? What are you doing lying there?

Me? I'm just here, making some thoughts.

What do you mean, *making* thoughts? You don't *make* thoughts.

You might not. I do.

Really? Like what?

Well, right now, for example, I'm thinking that dogs are truly contemptible animals, as well as being dangerous, and that they should be wiped out.

A very profound thought, I said with forced sarcasm. What else?

I've also made the thought that Italian politics are ridiculous; that stray cats can turn violent in spite of being almost always good-natured, fiercely independent beings; that abusive couples aren't at all uncommon; that people are obliging due to fear; that lots of primary school teachers are cruel; that *The Little Prince* is a book for kitsch forty-somethings; and that it doesn't make sense to have so many saints in the Gregorian calendar.

Ah, I said, or perhaps I didn't. Perhaps I only sighed. Or maybe I just breathed.

I also think, for example, that the fact that you've forgotten to get the car has to do with Bacon's parable of the horse's teeth.

Another parable?

Shut up and pay attention:

In the year of our Lord 1432, there arose a grievous quarrel among the brethren over the number of teeth in the mouth of a horse. For thirteen days the disputation raged without ceasing. All the ancient books and chronicles were fetched out, and wonderful and ponderous erudition such as was never before heard of in this region was made manifest. At the beginning of the fourteenth day, a youthful friar of goodly bearing asked his learned superiors for permission to add a word, and straightway, to the wonderment of the disputants, whose deep wisdom he sore vexed, he beseeched them to unbend in a manner coarse and unheard of and to look in the open mouth of a horse and find the answer to their questionings. At this, their dignity being grievously hurt, they waxed exceeding wroth; and, joining in a mighty uproar, they flew upon him and smote him, hip and thigh, and cast him out forthwith. For, said they, surely Satan hath tempted this bold neophyte to declare unholy and unheard-of ways of finding truth, contrary to all the teachings of the fathers. After many days more of grievous strife, the dove of peace sat on the assembly, and they as one man declaring the problem to be an everlasting mystery because of a grievous dearth of historical and theological evidence thereof, so ordered the same writ down.

I didn't understand a word of that, I said.

Don't you think it's fishy?

In what way?

In the way that you're a toothless, despicable, old man who doesn't understand, and forgets things and people.

Maybe you're right, I said, feeling the shrine to guilt carving out a larger space for itself somewhere in my chest.

And are you going to fetch my car now, small, insignificant, spindle-legged, deceitful, mediocre Fancioulle?

Well, maybe.

The clown said nothing—and his silence went on long enough for me to understand that our conversation had come to an end. Perhaps he was right. Maybe I should go and buy the makeup remover and get the car out of the pound. Anyway, I had nothing else to do. But what an idiotic thought. The clowns were just videos, and the voice was clearly coming in through the loudspeaker from somewhere else. I decided to wait patiently for the voice to sound again.

The first time I felt horror in the presence of a clown was at the age of fifteen or sixteen. I was in Balderas metro station with my friend El Perro. It was just after eleven at night, and we were coming back from playing dominoes on a friend's rooftop in downtown Mexico City. There was no one else in the station, just El Perro and I, waiting for the last train. At some point, we heard a sort of deep grunting sound, immediately followed by a huff. And again: grunt, huff, grunt. We looked around us—nothing, not a single soul in the station. El Perro went over and looked up the stairs connecting the platforms with the concourse. He stood there for a moment, frozen in astonishment. Then he beckoned me over and put his finger to his lips to indicate that I do so in silence. I moved cautiously toward him. Squatting on the top step, his pants at half-mast, a clown was taking a leisurely shit. I tried to stifle the laugh I felt rising up through my lungs like a nervous reflux, but was too slow. I emitted a sort of sneeze: a laugh passed through the muffler of self-constraint. The clown raised his head and looked into my eyes—he seemed to me like a defenseless animal looking straight at a possible predator, quickly realizing that the stalker is, in fact, its prey. He pulled up his pants and lunged at us. We ran, faster than we had ever before.

Terrified and disoriented, we retraced our path through the labyrinth of passages in Balderas station, looking for an unlocked exit. Rounding the corner of one passage, the clown came within grabbing distance and tackled me. I fell to the ground. He threw himself onto me, like a man throws himself onto a woman who is resisting him. Pinning me down by my lower legs, the clown let his head fall and pushed it into my belly, his button nose embedding itself in my navel. He buried his makeup-plastered face in my white shirt and, to my surprise, burst into tears—I never knew if from shame or natural sadness.

A few seconds later, having gotten my breath back, I

managed to slide from under his exhausted body, and El Perro and I continued on—now slowly and in silence—through the empty passages, until we found a way out that was open. End of memory.

For a long time, we made all kinds of jokes about that day, and told increasingly exaggerated versions of the story to our acquaintances. But beneath the laughter and buffoonery accompanying the anecdote, I felt a hot weight in my stomach every time the topic came up. I suppose the embers of humiliation I discovered burning in that clown's eyes had never left me.

After a while, the same lethargic, nasal voice sounded from the loudspeaker.

The great Fancioulle! It said, oozing with snide humor.

I assumed that the clown on my left was now addressing me, the one with the multiple ascending eyebrows.

I know what you're thinking, great, great Fancioulle.

What?

You're thinking you're better than the rest of us.

No, that's not so.

Have you heard the parable of the red-haired man, by the great writer and philosopher Daniil Kharms?

I have, in fact.

Well, you're like the red-haired man he wrote about, Fancioulle, so listen carefully:

> There was once a red-haired man who had no eyes or ears.
> Nor did he have any hair, so he was only red-haired on a

theoretical level. He couldn't speak, because he didn't have a mouth either. Nor did he have a nose. He didn't even have arms or legs. He had no stomach, no shoulders, no dorsal spine, and no intestines at all. The man had nothing! Hence, there is no way of knowing of whom we are talking. In fact, it would be better to say nothing else about him.

End of story.

End of story?

End of story.

That's not a parable. It's an allegory.

It's a superb parable, a supraparable, and one that seems inspired by your very self, Fancioulle. What do you think?

It's informative.

Really? Just informative?

Very informative, and also ingenious. But I don't understand why it's a parable.

And so what would you suggest I do about it, great Fancioulle?

I wouldn't suggest anything.

That's what I thought. Don't you realize that you've got nothing to offer?

Yes, I guess I do.

And that the schism between the perception you have of yourself and the perception other people have of you is irreconcilable?

Maybe.

You're also incapable of laughing at a joke that isn't your own. You're incapable of appreciating humor. And that reveals the limitations of your intelligence.

Fine.

And if you cross the boundaries of eccentricity, Fancio-ulle, what's on the other side is buffoonery: you're a clown.

Please, enough is enough.

That's just what I say, Fancioulle. Enough is enough. And if you did me a favor?

What is it?

I need a monograph on the Russian Revolution. Will you get it from the stationery store for me?

Yes, of course, I replied, suddenly finding myself swamped in docility.

And I need "Cotton and Its Derivatives" and "Arctic and Antarctic," plus one called "Whales and Their Derivatives," and maybe also "Flags of Asia."

o.k., I'll find them for you.

Thanks, replied the voice, satisfied.

By the way, you don't happen to know what model his vw is, do you? I inquired, pointing to the clown in the red bodysuit, who was looking at me in complete silence, blinking from time to time.

A white vw70, there's no doubt about it.

And which pound is it in?

I think it must be in the one over in Calle Ferrocaril. But why are you going for his car?

Because it was my fault they towed it away.

I waited for the clown's reply. It didn't come for some time. When the ventriloquist voice sounded again, I immediately knew that it was the fourth clown talking to me, the one with the sinister face painted red and black. I was by then prepared for the blows, the humiliation, for his outrageous attempts to wear me down. What that son of a fat sow didn't know is that the peerless Highway is unconfoundable and unbreakable. I decided to get in first, matching my face and voice to my predicament.

Fancioulle, at your service. What can I get you, Siddhartha?

There was a long silence.

What would you like, son? I repeated.

Nothing, he eventually replied.

No, really. What can I get you?

Nothing, really, nothing.

Come on, tell me. Something, anything at all, I insisted.

Honestly, you can't get me anything, sir.

A glass of water, at least?

No.

You're not going to refuse a glass of water!

Well, o.k. A glass of water.

I'll fetch it for you, I said, finally getting up from the floor and stretching my arms and legs. It took me a few moments to regain my balance, but as soon as I felt steady in my shoes, I crossed the room in a state of sudden, unconcealed euphoria. I felt light, freed of something. I suppose my uncle Fredo Sánchez Dostoyevsky was right when he said that insult, after all, is a purification of the soul. I made a polite bow to the catatonic clowns and went out the door: la-la-tra, la-la-tra.

对於從來沒有哲學家，可以耐心地忍受牙痛。

[There never existed a philosopher who could bear the pain of a toothache with patience.]

BOOK IV

The Circulars

Rigidity in the strict sense means naming the same thing at all worlds, or at least all worlds where that thing exists. That's all very well for numerals and the like, but without overlap of worlds we wouldn't expect an ordinary proper name of a person or a thing—of a railway, say—to be strictly rigid. However, an ordinary proper name may well be *quasi-rigid:* that is, it might name at another world the counterpart there of what it names here.

—DAVID LEWIS

I HAVE TO REPORT THAT ONE MORNING, I DON'T KNOW at what precise time, I too went out into the street after having passed a day and a night in my "room of ghosts," as my uncle Roberto Sánchez Walser used to call his sitting room. I'd lost my teeth, I'd slept on a bench, I'd allowed myself to be humiliated and emotionally tortured by my own son, but, despite all this, I was in an outlandish, tropically romantic-adventurer frame of mind; I believe that this is because I have always been a well-grounded person.

In the metallic light reflected by the clouds, I recognized the first signs of dawn and was relieved to find that I was in familiar surroundings: one of the parking lots of the old juice factory in Ecatepec, a few meters from the Vía Morelos. It had been raining and the air smelled of trailers, tortillas, and burnt tires. This is where I belong, I thought, and I remembered that masterly song by Napoleón, "Just for being what you are, that is why I love you." It made me want to sing out loud at the top of my voice, and that's what I did.

I crossed the grounds of the factory, singing beneath the wiry early morning clouds, until I came to a bicycle shelter. Among the workers arriving at the factory, stopping off at the shelter to leave their vehicles, I spotted my wise old friend Tacito—who writes Chinese fortune cookie proverbs for a living—attempting to chain a bicycle to one of the metal tubes. He was wrapped in an ivory-colored toga, his hair neatly combed and his mustache cut painter's-brush style—as elegant and distinguished as ever. He greeted me effusively and asked how I was, but when I opened my mouth to answer him, he noticed my missing teeth and couldn't hide his shock.

Quid accidit, Highway?

As you see, my dear friend, I said. I've lost my teeth.

E longinquo contemplari, si non nocet, he responded with his accustomed serenity.

Thank you. I think that son of a bitch of my son stole them, I said. But I'm not sure. I'm going to go looking for them.

Cum cœperint cum faciunt animos nostros facultas amittatur.

Exactly, my dear friend. Listen, could you lend me your bicycle to search for them?

He told me that the bicycle belonged to his brother, and then asked me if I had happened to come across him. I replied no, I hadn't seen him in many years. His brother, it seemed, had taken an almost lethal dose of peyote a week before and had wandered off into the streets of Ecatepec. Tacito had been looking for him for several days in order to return his bicycle. I am practical. I proposed a sensible solution:

Instead of chaining it up, why not let me borrow the bicycle, and I'll look for your brother while I'm trying to find my teeth?

Tacito, in turn, has always been reasonable and generous.

Et spes inanes, et velut somnia quaedam, vigilantium, Highway my friend, he said, offering me the handlebars.

Then, from a leather satchel he had strapped diagonally across his chest, he took a bag of Chinese fortune cookies and placed them in the basket of the bicycle with a solemn gesture:

Antiquam sapientiam Chinese fortune cookies vestram in comitetur vobiscum quaerere.

I thanked him sincerely and mounted the bicycle. Then I crossed Morelos and turned into Sonora, heading east, determined to fulfill all my tasks, possibly find Tacito's lost brother, and even perhaps recover my teeth. A wide, clear sky was before me, and the sun was just beginning to show itself among the stark rebars on the housetops.

At that time of day, the only place open was Las Explicaciones, on the corner of Sonora and Las Torres. It's famous because the coffee costs one peso, a round of bread five, and there are always several copies of that day's paper. I stopped off for breakfast and asked for a newspaper, and a Nescafé to wet the Chinese fortune cookies Tacito had given me. I extracted the slips of paper on which the fortunes were written and then dunked and soaked each cookie until it was just soggy enough for me to swallow without fear of damaging my bare gums. The slips I put in my trouser pocket for later.

Besides myself, the only other customer in the café was a slender, circumspect young man, his face speckled with tobacco-colored freckles, deep in concentration. He was wearing a bright yellow three-piece suit that was too big for him and a Panama hat. Seated at a table by a window through which the early morning light was beginning to enter, he was holding a pencil and silently writing in a notebook.

From my table, I asked what it was he was writing so much about. His eyes still on the notebook, he said he was just planning a relingo walk.

A *what* walk? I burbled in my newly acquired toothless old fool voice.

A walk around gaps, sir, around vacant lots, spaces without owners or fixed use, he clarified with those three elucidations.

I opened my mouth like a newly hatched chick, and, pointing to my edentate cavern, I said:

Empty spaces like this one?

The youth raised his eyes, finally interested in me. I took advantage of his attention to continue, being careful not to lose that interest:

What's your name?

Jacobo de Voragine. But they call me Voragine.

What are you? A singer-songwriter? An artist?

No, he said in a melodramatic tone. I'm a writer and church tour guide in the city. I live by the latter and die by the former.

Ah! So you must know the writer who wrote a book and changed his teeth.

No, sir. Who's he?

A writer who had all his teeth replaced after writing a book, that's all.

Fabulous. Fascinating. Amazing, he said hesitatingly, unsure of his adjectives.

And by the way, Gustavo Sánchez Sánchez, or just Highway, at your service. Would you mind if I came and sat there in the sun with you? I don't want to break your concentration.

Of course, be my guest, please take a seat; in any case, I haven't had a single idea all morning.

I ordered three more Nescafés—two for me and one for him—and sat down opposite the young man. His bony hands were tipped, I noted, with the short nails of the nervous.

So you're a newcomer to the neighborhood?

That's right, sir.

And how do you intend to be a tour guide here if you don't know the place?

No, the tourists don't come here. I live in Ecatepec, but I give guided walking tours in the center of Mexico City.

Do you live alone?

No, with two brothers who work in the book trade. I don't know their names, but between themselves they call each other Darling and Understanding, without distinction. They own a printing press and publisher called Rincón Cultural.

And why do you think you haven't been able to write today?

I don't know. Perhaps it's because I'm terrified of irrelevance.

Irrelevance?

There are already too many things—he went on in the tone of the chronically ill—too many books, too many opinions. Anything I do will only add to the great pile of trash every person leaves behind him. Am I making sense?

Perfect sense. That's why I'm an auctioneer.

You? You auction works of art?

Anything that comes my way.

For example?

For example, I can auction you my name. I've collected six homonyms. I call the series "Circular Gustavos," because they have to be auctioned through riddled circumlocutions, like Statius's epithets and periphrases.

How so?

So:

Pisces, Scorpio ascendant. Born in San Andrés, Chalchicamula, March 18, 1911. He was president of Mexico from 1964 to 1970, during which time he: disappeared students, militarily occupied the National Autonomous University of Mexico, imprisoned workers, sacked teachers, doctors, and railway men who were protesting about low wages. He died of colorectal cancer.

Who is it? I asked Voragine.

No idea, Highway. Sorry.

President Gustavo Díaz-Ordaz, of course. Let's try another.

Born on April 19, 1801, under the sign of Taurus, Libra ascendant. Originator of the study of psychophysics and a visionary pioneer of experimental psychology. He also discovered the famous formula $S = K \ln I$, which describes the nonlinear relationship between psychological sensations and impressions and the intensity of physical stimuli. Active, atheist, womanizer, and a good-hearted man, he died on November 18, 1887.

Who am I referring to?
Sorry, no idea.
Gustav Theodor Fechner. Another:

Sagittarius, writer, fat, French.

Oh! Gustav Flaubert?
Yes, indeed.
O.K., give me another.
O.K.:

Cancer, Aquarius ascendant. He was born on July 7, 1860, and died May 18, 1911. Jewish, a native of Bohemia, he composed Mahler's Symphonies, 1-10 but didn't complete the tenth because he died before it was finished. He was married to Mrs. Alma Mahler, who also had relations with Walter Gropius, Franz Werfel, Klimt, Max Burkhard, Alexander von Zemlinsky, Oskar Kokoshka, and Johannes Hollsteiner, to name but a few.

Easy: Gustav Mahler.
Good, good. Another:

Sagittarius. She was a feminist born in Hamburg in 1868.

Is that all the information?
Yes, sorry.

I don't know.

It's Lida Gustava Heymann. I'll give you one last one:

> Cancer, Cancer ascendant. An astrological disaster. Lover and possible husband of Gustav Mahler's wife. He was a symbolist painter prone to cluster migraines and erotic expression.

Gustav Klimt?

Correct.

Amusing, he said. But how do you auction the names?

I just do. What auctioneers auction, in the end, are just names of people, and maybe words. All I do is give them new content.

Explain?

You see, I'm like those people who scavenge in your garbage. But with pedigree. I expurgate; I find. I aromatize, clean, and disinfect. I recycle.

Young Jacobo de Voragine stared at his, as yet untouched, cup of Nescafé. He picked up the dispenser, tipped a disgusting quantity of sugar into the cup, and, using his pencil, stirred the coffee in a desultory fashion.

Let's see. Read me what you're writing now, I said, trying to keep the conversation alive.

But it's nothing special, just a description of a corner.

I remained silent, waiting for him to begin. The young man hesitated for a moment, but then opened his notebook, cleared his throat, and read:

> There's a hardware store opposite the house I've moved into. I can see it from the window of the bathroom on the

roof, the only place where I can smoke in silence. Every afternoon, while the men who serve in the hardware store are beginning to close up, the owner, a senile man, takes a folding chair out onto the sidewalk and starts sharpening the ends of the tacks that he has in a toolbox next to the leg of the chair. One by one, he sharpens them carefully on the curbside, and then throws them into the street. The ritual lasts no more than ten minutes. I flick my cigarette into the toilet and he folds up his chair.

That's as far as I've got, he said, with a look that begged for approval.

It's tender, I said.

Thanks.

And you have nice, small handwriting.

Thanks.

But it's all wrong.

Why, sir?

It's about Mr. Alfonso Reyes's hardware store, right? La Higuera. The one on the corner of Durango and Morelos.

How could you tell?

Ah, little bird, that's a long story. But the point is that your description is inaccurate, because Mr. Alfonso is not gaga and neither is he sharpening those tacks. He blunts them. He blunts the ones that are a bit bent, and, when they're properly blunt, he throws them into the street so that they don't burst tires or bugger up cars.

And why doesn't he throw them in the trash?

Because they rip the bags.

I see.

Look Jacobo, Voragine, young Jacobo Voragine, I think I can help you if you help me. You know, you scratch my back, I'll scratch yours.

I'm not sure if I can help you, sir; I'm not good for much. But go on.

I need to recover my dignities—my teeth, that is—because I can't recycle anything without them, let alone eat or speak like a human being. And you lack money, time, freedom, peace, work experience, street life, women, stimulants, and everything you surely need for your masterpieces.

That's true, sir.

But you can't have any of that. You can't, because you commute two hours every day to grimy downtown Mexico City, where you work for some son of a bitch who exploits you, and you go back to your apartment, where other young men like you live—all dressed up just as strangely—and the house is a pigsty, so you start washing the dishes, sweeping up the hairballs on the floor, folding T-shirts, hanging up odd socks. You make yourself a sandwich with just cheese, because the ham has all gone snotty green, and by the end of the day, you're so tired and depressed that you've lost the will to sit down and do the one thing you love.

I'm speechless, Mr. Highway. How did you know about the hairballs?

I'm no babe in arms.

So I see. But I still don't understand what you're getting at, sir.

That you become a real artist.

And how do you suggest I do that? he asked, in an almost crotchety voice, straightening his hat.

That's where I come in. I can give you a lot of things, like free lodging, for example. An artist needs free lodging. I have a mansion in Calle Disneylandia, with the best collection of objects that's ever been seen. And don't go thinking I'm some sort of degenerate like Michael Jackson. I like ladies my own age.

Free lodging? And what else?

I can give you an education.

Such as?

Such as how to avoid paying for your meals, or how to ride buses for free. I can also give you street. I know this neighborhood better than anyone, and I can give you all that knowledge. This is how it will work: I tell you the story of every corner; I introduce you to my contacts; I take you under my wing, as they say. In time, when you really know this place, you can open your own tourist business here. End of story.

And where do I find the tourists?

They'll come on their own. The important thing is to tell stories about the neighborhood. As soon as you've got those, there'll be people flocking to hear them. Places and things are made up of stories.

I'm not so sure about that.

Isn't telling stories what you do?

Yes.

Well, have a bit of faith, won't you?

Let's suppose you're right. That I say yes to your proposal. What are you going to ask me to do in return?

Almost nothing. You just write for me.

Write what?

Whatever I commission you to do. First I need you to write my story, the story of my teeth. I tell it to you, you just write it. We sell millions, and I get my teeth fixed for good. Then, when I die, you write about that too. Because a man's story is never complete until he dies. End of that task.

And what else?

Well, then, if we rub along well together, I can offer you other jobs.

Such as?

Such as, I need someone to catalog my collection of collectibles. Because I auction only my own collections now. I've got the world's best collection. And as I haven't got much longer in this world, I want to hold a grand auction, for which I need a catalog. But let's not jump the gun. For the time being, you just write my dental autobiography.

The melancholy young Voragine finally smiled, but he made no reply.

What are you smiling at?

Nothing. That it would be your biography, not your autobiography.

Ah! I see that you're going to be a good writer too.

Why do you say that?

Because when you smile, you don't show your teeth. Real writers never show their teeth. Charlatans, in contrast, flash that sinister crescent when they smile. Check it out. Find photos of all the writers you respect, and you'll see that their teeth remain a permanently occult mystery.

I believe the only exception is the Argentinian Jorge Francisco Isidoro Luis.

Borges?

The selfsame. Blind and Argentinian. But he doesn't count because he was blind, so he probably couldn't picture himself smiling—at least, not with the smile he had when he was blind, if you know what I mean.

Borges is my idol. Have you read him? asked young Voragine with childlike enthusiasm.

Not as much as I will in the future, I replied.

I think you and I are going to rub along well, Mr. Highway. And I'd be happy to write your biography.

It is my autobiography, you stubborn matchstick, because it is my story, and I will tell it, you'll just transcribe.

As you wish, sir. I'd be happy to write your dental autobiography.

That's more like it.

We spent the rest of the morning ordering Nescafés, exchanging stories, and fine-tuning the details of our arrangement. Around noon, the summer sun began to warm the concrete floor of the café. The Nescafés had us as perky as a couple of protococaine addicts, and the Chinese fortune cookies had all gone.

Let's go, Voragine, I said, leaving a twenty on the table, Benito Juarez face up. I've got my new bicycle here outside. A friend just gave it to me.

My bicycle's outside too, he said.

Perfect. We can pick up your things and I'll take you to Disneylandia.

I'm in.
Great. Say no more. Shall we go?
Right now?
This very instant.

End of conversation.

TACITO'S FORTUNE COOKIES:

該名男子在山頂不降

The man atop the mountain does not fall.

龍仍然在深水變成獵物的螃蟹。

The motionless dragon in deep waters
becomes the prey of the crabs.

福无重至,禍不单行

Fortune never comes with a parallel, and misfortune never comes alone.

當兩兄弟一起工作的山區轉向黃金。

When two brothers work together, the mountains turn to gold.

不聞不若聞之, 聞之不若見之, 見之不若知之, 知之不若行之; 學至於行之而止矣

Not hearing is not as good as hearing, hearing is not as good
as seeing, seeing is not as good as mentally knowing, mentally
knowing is not as good as acting; true learning continues up to the
point of action.

風向轉變時,有人築牆,有人造風車

When the wind changes, some people build walls, others windmills.

舌頭抗拒, 因為它是軟的, 牙齒產生, 因為他們是很難的。

The tongue resists because it is soft; the teeth yield
because they are hard.

把話說到心窩裡

Put your words in the mouth of the stomach.

BOOK V

The Allegorics

My speculations led me to conclude that I had to go back to basics and rethink not just the semantics of names, but their very syntax, the metaphysics of words: How should words be individuated? What is the nature of a word?

Names are a special kind of word, so special that some have thought them not to be a part of a language at all. I disagree with this and will emphasize ways in which names are like other words, but I do not disagree that names are special in several ways.

——DAVID KAPLAN

I AM NOT SURE IF THIS SHOULD BE IN THE STORY, BECAUSE it's a part that seems to start folding over on itself, so that I become confused and agitated and lose my way. But I don't see how it can be ignored either.

When Voragine and I got back to Disneylandia, we found that my house and warehouse had been broken into. My collection was gone, every single item. I first felt tremendous relief. Then, a little sadness. Then disbelief, and anger. Then, again, a deeper form of sadness and relief fused together, almost a weightlessness.

The following days were confusing and difficult, and I'd rather not speak about them. I attended group therapy. I watched Formula 1. I considered Catholicism. I was lost like a swallow in Antarctica, as Napoleón says.

One morning, while we were drinking coffee, Voragine tried to persuade me to go to the dentist and get a temporary set of dentures, so I could at least begin eating proper food. I resisted a little, but the boy was right, and I'm a reasonable man despite a certain stubbornness. As soon as I'd gotten the new dentures—cheap and a bit too tight, but functional—I began dictating my dental autobiography.

It took me some time to find the right structures, but Voragine pointed out that there should be a beginning, a middle, and an end, and that helped me to get started.

A month later, as I had promised him, we began the "Education of the Voragine Artist." Our first lesson: to pick up and recycle some objects that my son left for me in the gallery next to the juice factory. Around one in the morning on a particularly quiet Sunday, my friend El Perro, who still worked as a driver for the factory, came to pick us up in a handsome truck. We took the back road, where there wasn't a single security checkpoint. El Perro parked in an alley, handed me a set of keys, and Voragine and I went into the small building adjacent to the factory, where the gallery is located. We started in the office to the right of the entrance of the gallery. We didn't find much there, but Voragine took a catalog from the desk, which later came in handy. I requisitioned some pencils, which would also come in handy, as Voragine was doing a lot of writing.

We walked around carefully, because the gallery was quite dark, and we'd decided not to turn the main lights on, in case there were cameras. The only illumination came from the spots directed onto the objects. I have to say that, in this particular light, they looked more beautiful than I remembered from when I had first seen them on the morning of my brief captivity. I first recognized the plush costumes, the musical score on its podium, the prosthetic leg.

I am not the crying sort, not even in movies. When I suddenly saw my old teeth—the ones that I'd sold off at the auction in the church—I didn't cry. I neighed with joy. They were arranged in a little pile, lit vertically from above, and placed on a white wooden pedestal. They were truly something. I gathered them together with my two hands and placed them in my jacket pocket.

The rest of the operation went quickly and smoothly. The only object that gave us any trouble was the medium-sized billboard with a horse, but together we managed to drag it to the truck, and El Perro helped us to get it inside. A couple of hours later, the three of us were back in my warehouse, studying the new collection of objects and swigging from a bottle of Aguardiente, which El Perro had contributed. "Better the lucky man than the lucky man's son," El Perro said before he fell asleep in the Acapulco chair. You can't help but love a man like that.

The following morning I woke Voragine at 7:00 a.m. and led him to the kitchen. El Perro had gone home—he's a man who never gives others trouble. I handed my young apprentice a cup of coffee and a series of Scribe notebooks. I'd had a good idea for an auction, and good ideas don't come on wheels, so I wanted to get it down on paper immediately.

The series would be called "Allegorics of Ecatepec," and would recycle our new collected objects by telling stories that used collected names of my friends and acquaintances from the neighborhood—giving due credits to the artists who had made the works and using the catalog we had requisitioned as our guide. No complications. The best ideas, like the finest objects, are simple.

But if we use the artists' real names, Voragine said, we'll get caught.

Yes, good thinking young man. We will have to modify them.

But if we modify them, he went on, the objects will lose their value.

No, they won't.

Yes, they will.

Voragine, please shut up and write this down:

ALLEGORIC LOT NO. 1: BILLBOARD FEATURING HORSE
ARTIST: DOUG SÁNCHEZ AITKEN

LISTING: 1M

Everyone knows that horses have no compassion, I told Alan Pauls. If a horse sees you standing in front of it, crying, it just chews its hay and blinks. You start crying harder, your eyes overflowing with tears and pain, and the horse lifts its tail and lets out a long, silent fart. There is no way to stir its feelings. I once dreamed that a horse was persistently licking my face. But that doesn't count, because it happened in a dream.

I can assure you that the horses working in Central Park on the island of Manhattan suffer from depression, Alan Pauls responded after I'd ventured to propose my theory to him. We were both waiting for the bus, next to Rubén Darío Jr.'s newspaper stand. I noticed that Alan Pauls was contemplating, with a tinge of melancholy, the spectacular hoarding before us, on the other side of the street. On it was an advertisement with a photo of a horse—perhaps, indeed, a rather sad horse—standing next to a bed in a New York hotel.

And how do you know that the horses in Central Park are depressed?

He told me that he'd just been reading a short article on the psychology of New York horses.

In which newspaper? I challenged.

He had read it in the newspaper he'd bought at the stand. He had it in his briefcase if I happened to be interested—it's from one of those cheap but trustworthy publications, he explained. The horses in New York's Central Park, the reporter of the free but reliable newspaper had said, get depressed.

And how do they know? I asked.

There's empirical, scientific proof, he said, his patience perhaps wearing a little thin. Then he took the newspaper out of his briefcase, opened it, and searched for the article. He quickly located it and began to read aloud, making opportune pauses and raising his eyes every so often to meet mine and to check that I was giving him my full attention. The horses of that city: 1) run at full speed and smash their muzzles and heads against the walls of buildings; 2) have manes that fall out in handfuls; 3) bite their hooves until they fall off; 4) defecate lying down instead of while walking, as all *normal* horses do; 5) some, eventually, commit suicide.

When he had finished reading the short article, he folded the newspaper again and settled it under his arm. He smiled vaguely at me. We went on waiting for the bus together, silently staring at the billboard on the other side of the street.

ALLEGORIC LOT NO. 2: WINDOW MADE OF LIGHT

ARTIST: OLAFUR SÁNCHEZ ELIASSON

LISTING: 5M

The retired seamstress Margo Glantz didn't wake her son until after dinner. During the preceding week, Margo Glantz, who suffered from insomnia, had been feeling irritated by the presence of her son, David Miklos, who, for his part, suffered from narcolepsy. David Miklos had lost his job at the checkout in the Farmacia del Ahorro because he'd fallen asleep on more than one occasion. For the last week, he'd spent the whole day taking sudden naps in odd corners of the house. Since she wasn't aware of his condition, Margo Glantz considered him to be an idler, a layabout, and a sluggard. Secretly, she envied his ability to sleep at any hour of the day.

On Monday afternoon, while David Miklos was having another inopportune nap in the armchair, Margo Glantz stuck a row of postage stamps on his forehead, licking each one with the tip of her tongue, and carried him to the post office. She set him down gently on the counter and asked the assistant to send him to Surinam. The girl looked down her nose at her and said that it was impossible to carry out her request as she was four stamps short—Africa needed nine stamps and the parcel only had five.

But Surinam's in South America, you idiot, she retorted.

Then it's twelve stamps, corrected the girl.

She also said that the post office was about to close, so she would have to come back the following day.

Margo Glantz returned the next day and the next, with David Miklos sleeping peacefully in her arms. But she always needed something else—a stamp, a notarized letter for oversized packages, more money, official identification, the full zip code for the address she had given in Paramaribo. The girl—who, though not the same one each time, appeared to be so due to the robotic demeanor and characteristic affectation of all post-office girls—would give her a disparaging look and ask her to come back the following day.

On the morning of the seventh day, a Sunday, Margo Glantz decided to let David Miklos sleep on. She woke up early, had a warm bath, and went to the pet shop. As there were no dogs for sale, she made do with a secondhand rabbit. She named it Cockerspaniel. The rabbit was very old, almost venerable, so when she tried to put a lead on it to take it out of the store, it resisted. She carried it home in her arms and set it down on the living room floor, at the foot of the armchair in which David Miklos was still sleeping.

Margo Glantz—slowly, and making as much noise as possible—dragged a chair from the kitchen to the living room. She put on a record by the singer Taylor Mac, sat down, crossed her legs, and, singing at the top of her voice, stared at Cockerspaniel, who in turn looked at her with an air of extreme peevishness until he closed his eyes and fell into a deep sleep. She noticed that Cockerspaniel had chosen a sunny patch of floor to sleep in and felt intensely envious. She thought about taking him straight to the post office and sending him to Surinam—or wherever. But she immediately rejected the idea when she remembered that the disgusting, ridiculous, inefficient post office didn't open on Sundays. Later, she attempted to wake the rabbit, but he just briefly fluttered an eyelid and went back to sleep.

The afternoon went by with Margo Glantz watching her son and Cockerspaniel sleep, noting how the animal's small, furry body slid almost imperceptibly across the room as the sun sank in the sky and the parallelogram of light entering through the window and falling onto the floor moved toward the wall, indicating, in this way, the passage of the hours.

When the sun had finally set, and the patch of light had completely disappeared, Cockerspaniel opened his eyes. Margo Glantz was standing above him, holding a saucepan by the handle. Using the base of the pan, she hit him five times on the head. Once Cockerspaniel was dead, she carefully skinned the rabbit and cooked it in rosemary, bay leaf, and white wine. After she'd finished her dinner, she tenderly woke her son and opened the living room window wide, letting in the cool, damp night air.

ALLEGORIC LOT NO. 3: RAT AND MOUSE COSTUMES
ARTIST: PETER SÁNCHEZ FISCHLI
LISTING: 3M

The young lady Valeria Luiselli, a mediocre high school student, stammered and overused the suffix -ly. As her parents, Mrs. Weiss and Mr. Fischli, wanted her to give a speech at her fifteenth birthday party, they sent her to singing, elocution, and public speaking classes. Her party was to be a very elegant celebration in the neighborhood dancehall, and the girl needed to prepare herself for the occasion.

For the elocution and public speaking classes, they hired the famous teacher Guillermo Sheridan. The first sentence that Professor Guillermo Sheridan taught Valeria Luiselli to say was: "Titus Livy had a conk like a coconut and Octavio Paz was a big head." Despite the shortness and simplicity of the sentence, it took the young girl a lot of effort to pronounce it correctly. Every time she made a mistake, Professor Guillermo Sheridan would hit her on the palm of the hand with a cane. The girl had to repeat the same sentence 112 times before her teacher called an end to the first session.

That night, while they were eating a dinner of octopus a la gallega with white rice, the girl's parents asked her how her first public speaking class had gone, and if she had learned anything useful that she would like to share with them. The young girl said:

Titus Livy was a cokehead.

What's that, my girl? asked her father.

Titus Livy was a cokehead, repeated the adolescent.

Valeria Luiselli's parents looked each other in the eyes and ate the rest of their octopus in silence.

That night, the young girl's progenitors put on their plush rat and mouse costumes, and, instead of reading or watching television, as they did almost every other night, they committed an act of outlandish, noisy, uninterrupted coitus. When they had finished, still half-dressed in their costumes, the couple lay silently staring at the ceiling.

ALLEGORIC LOT NO. 4: SHIT MOUNTAIN
ARTIST: DAMIÁN SÁNCHEZ ORTEGA
LISTING: 4M

Yuri Herrera, captain of the Alpha Patrol, was voted best traffic policewoman in 2011. One sleepless Sunday night, Captain Yuri Herrera memorized the whole of the famous speech from *Macbeth* that begins, "Tomorrow and tomorrow and tomorrow . . ." She recited it in front of the mirror one last time at 5:25 a.m. while arranging her hair into a bun, held in place by a number of bobby pins and barrettes. Then she put her whistle between her teeth and blew.

She went out into the street looking impeccable. As she was turning the corner of Amapola and Amapolas, she met her fellow policewoman, Vivian Abenshushan, the Omega Patrol's hostage negotiator.

What've we got today, Abenshushan? she asked.

The 10-14 in Avenida Morelos in 11-27 toward Parque del Amor, partner. We're just in time.

Captain Abenshushan was taller and stronger than Captain Herrera, but they were equally valiant.

At that moment, Terence Gower and Rubén Gallo, owners of the Couscous & Chopsticks public sauna, came by, mounted on identical bicycles, and waved to the two policewomen. The officers straightened their shoulders, smiled, and returned the greeting by blowing their whistles. At that moment, the 10-14 passed, wound down the window of his brown Nissan Tsuru, and threw an empty plastic bottle in their direction. The bottle fell at Captain Abenshushan's feet, and, furious, she kicked it as hard as she could into the street. Thanks to the friendly cyclists, they had, once again, failed to apprehend the 10-14 who chucked an empty Coke bottle at them every morning.

My life is a mountain of shit, said Captain Abenshushan in a slightly theatrical voice. Captain Yuri Herrera, who, being older, was better prepared to resist the blows of another day, identical to the one before and the one to come and the one after that, recited to her partner, in the vehement, earnest tone only learned in the police academy, the Shakespearean monologue she'd memorized the night before.

Captain Abenshushan listened attentively, harboring

the vague suspicion that her partner was beginning to go soft in the head. But she immediately repressed this thought deep within her and blew her whistle twice, in a demonstration of gratitude for Captain Herrera's empathy. Feeling they deserved a break, Captains Herrera and Abenshushan decided to have breakfast at the gorditas stand owned by Toño Ortuño, Las Gorditas de Pancho Villa, on the corner of Isabel la Católica, in the hope that the morning would pass quickly.

ALLEGORIC LOT NO. 5: PROSTHETIC LEG
ARTIST: ABRAHAM CRUZVILLEGAS SÁNCHEZ
LISTING: 6M

One day Unamuno went to the store to buy hens' eggs. Unamuno didn't eat eggs, but his wife, who had a wooden leg, wanted to make an omelet and asked Unamuno to go to Daniel Saldaña París's store and buy eggs. She explicitly requested that they be white, not brown.

Unamuno came back from the store with a paper bag full of brown eggs. Looking into the bag and noting that the eggs were not the color she'd wanted, the woman shouted, Idiot! and made him go back to the store for white eggs.

Unamuno went back to the store, where, this time, he bought white eggs. When he returned home, he found his wife asleep on the bed. The woman had left her wooden leg leaning against the rolltop desk, as she always did when she took a midmorning nap.

Then, Unamuno placed the bag of eggs on the carpeted floor and, using the false leg, gave her six blows to wake her up.

ALLEGORIC LOT NO. 6: BAT

ARTIST: MIGUEL SÁNCHEZ CALDERÓN

LISTING: 6M

Guillermo Fadanelli was reading *The Phenomenology of Spirit* by a one-quarter namesake of his, Jorge Guillermo Federico Hegel, when suddenly a midget came into the Shanghai Star restaurant in which he was seated, pulled up a chair, and sat down opposite him. The man identified himself as Pushkin. They asked the waiter for a round of beers and Pushkin started to cry. The reason for his tears, he told Guillermo Fadanelli, was that his father was a rake. The word he used was донжуан, and it is not certain if the translation "rake" is correct.

Half an hour later, Pushkin took his leave. Immediately afterward, another midget entered the restaurant and came to sit at the table. Guillermo Fadanelli invited him to have a drink. After taking a handkerchief from his pocket, wiping away the tears streaming down his face, and noisily blowing his nose, the midget said that his name was Gogol and that the reason for his unhappiness was that he'd learned that his father was a degenerate. In this case, the word he used was вырождаться. Everything would appear to indicate that the translation "degenerate" is correct.

When Gogol left, a third midget came into the restaurant. Predictably, he repeated the same routine as his two predecessors and sat down at the table. Studying him as he blew his nose, Guillermo Fadanelli said: Let me guess, your name is Dostoyevsky, and you are wretched because your wife is a трутень. The midget stared at him in astonishment. Why do you say that? he asked, after taking a long swig of beer. Guillermo Fadanelli answered that догадался по горячности своего голоса and gave a slightly ironic smile. You're wrong, Guillermo. My name is Daniil Kharms, and I'm blowing my nose because I'm allergic to pollen.

At that moment, the waiter approached the table holding a basket of Chinese fortune cookies. Guillermo Fadanelli took one and split it into two halves the way you would crack an egg. He let the slip of paper fall onto the table. Then, slowly unfolding it, he read aloud:

℘ That is how one imagines the Bat of History. His face is turned toward the past. Where we perceive a chain of events, he sees a single catastrophe that piles ruin onto ruin and he hurls it to his feet. He would dearly like to stop, to awaken the dead and to reassemble what has been torn to shreds, but a hurricane is blowing in from Paradise and becomes tangled in his wings, forming a knot of brilliant lights, a knot so strong that the angel can no longer close its wings. This hurricane impels him inevitably toward the future, to which his back is turned, while the rubble rises up to the sky before him. That hurricane is what we call progress. (WALTER BENJAMIN, slightly changed.)

Does the slip of paper say all that? asked Daniil Kharms.

Yes, replied Guillermo Fadanelli.

I don't believe you, Kharms retorted, and shot Fadanelli between the eyes.

He then extracted a cookie from the basket the waiter was still holding out. Copying his now defunct companion's movements, he broke it into two identical halves, let the slip of paper fall onto the table, picked it up, and read:

℘ When biting bamboo sprouts with your teeth, remember the man who planted them.

ALLEGORIC NO. 7: BONSAI BAOBAB
ARTIST: SAM SÁNCHEZ DURANT
LISTING: 3.5M

Mario Levrero had had a lousy month. September was almost over and he hadn't been able to sell a single life insurance policy; apparently no one was afraid of death any longer. When he left his office, Every Minute Insurance, on Friday, he walked to Mr. Alejandro Zambra's nursery and bought a bonsai baobab tree. He was feeling so inadequate that he attempted to commit suicide by hanging himself from a branch of that tiny plant. He only just failed.

ALLEGORIC LOT NO. 8: STUFFED DOG
ARTIST: MAURIZIO SÁNCHEZ CATTELAN
LISTING: 2.3M

Some years ago, Álvaro Enrigue, the bus driver on route M100, treacherously attempted to run over a paralyzed old lady on Avenida Revolución. He served a brief but horrid sentence. After his release, I met him one afternoon in Mrs. Abramo's bar, Let There Be Lux, and he told me that on that fateful day, the notary, Juan José Arreola, had gotten on his bus at the corner of Loma Bonita and Avenida Interior. As soon as Álvaro Enrigue saw him, he knew his presence was an ill omen. In fact, at the next stop, a pair of identical twins in shirtsleeves, who identified themselves as Oscar de Pablo and Pedro de Pablo, lifted a lady in a wheelchair with a dog sleeping in her arms onto the bus. Between them, they hoisted her out of the wheelchair, settled her in the seat next to the notary, and got off the bus in silence. The dog continued to sleep like a baby in the old lady's flaccid arms.

Two blocks farther on, the lady asked for the next stop, saying: Stop. The same young men in shirtsleeves were waiting for her, holding the handles of the wheelchair. They boarded the bus, lifted the old lady, and, once outside, deposited her in the wheelchair again, with the dog still sleeping peacefully. A few blocks later, the same two men, with the same lady still sitting in her wheelchair, waved down the bus. They repeated the previous procedure, and, two blocks farther on, the lady again requested a stop by calling out: Stop.

During all this, the notary, Juan José Arreola, feigned exhaustion, incapable of saying or doing anything about the clearly absurd situation, as intolerable for the driver as for some of the passengers.

In Calle Barranca, Mr. Paco Goldman Molina and Mrs. Guadalupe Nettel boarded the bus. They took out their guitars and began to perform "La Guanábana." A slight smile appeared on Álvaro Enrigue's face. He turned right into Revolución and asked Paco and Guadalupe to do "La Baraja." While Paco Goldman sang and Guadalupe Nettel strummed her guitar, the ascent and descent of the paralyzed old lady and her sleeping dog was repeated yet again, with the assistance of the twins of ill omen.

Álvaro Enrigue had had enough. The half-empty glass of his proverbial Spartan patience had been drained. When the shirt-sleeved twins, standing on the corner of Revolución and Periodismo like a pair of malevolent sphinxes, next to the lady in the wheelchair and her disgustingly dormant dog, yet again waved down the bus, he drove it straight at the four of them. The twins and the old lady, who turned out to be not in the least paralyzed, managed to dodge the bus by throwing themselves to one side. The dog, however, was killed in the unfortunate mishap.

ALLEGORIC LOT NO. 9: MUSIC SCORE ON TRIPOD
ARTIST: FERNANDO SÁNCHEZ ORTEGA
LISTING: 3M

> Mario Bellatin and César Aira straightened their black
> jackets, adjusted their sunglasses, and looked attentively at
> the score in front of them. Taking one deep, synchronized
> breath, they began, in C major, "The Lord is my shepherd,
> I shall not want …"

End of Allegorics. When I'd finished dictating, I made a
repast of bread and tomato for Voragine and myself, and we
sat down in my Acapulco chairs to watch television. You
never know when society is going to make mountains out
of molehills. The news bulletin had all its alarm bells ring-
ing. A massive burglary had been reported at the gallery
belonging to the juice factory. The police had detained a
suspect, whose name they would not yet reveal, but who
was associated with the factory. Our first thought was to
fear for El Perro. Then, a little, for ourselves. But when I
rang him up, his wife said he was taking a nap. I was certain
they'd arrested Siddhartha.

And I was right, wasn't I, Voragine?

Yes, Highway, you were.

Nevertheless, we decided that we should get rid of the
lots as soon as possible. That night, we asked El Perro to help
us take them to Mr. Ibargüengoitia's junkyard, on Calle
Ferrocarril. We got one hundred pesos for them.

And I guess I can now say that I lived happily thereafter, right Voragine?

I guess, so, Highway.

So write that down and let's go out to meet some ladies.

會偷蛋，就會偷牛

[He who steals an egg will steal an ox.]

BOOK VI

The Elliptics

If "the author of *Waverley*" meant anything other than "Scott," "Scott is the author of *Waverley*" would be false, which it is not. If "the author of *Waverley*" meant "Scott," "Scott is the author of *Waverley*" would be a tautology, which it is not. Therefore, "the author of *Waverley*" means neither "Scott" nor anything else—i.e., "the author of *Waverley*" means nothing.

—BERTRAND RUSSELL

W HEN I FIRST KNEW HIGHWAY, HE WAS SICK AND
weak. Whenever he saw his reflection in a mirror, he
would say that he looked like a backyard hen and then cluck
at himself. Indeed, the little hair he had was permanently
sticking up heavenward; he had scrawny, veined legs, and
a rounded, bulging belly. He had lost his beloved false
teeth, so that such an ordinary thing as speaking was, if
not impossible, a constant battle against humiliation. But
Highway was a man of easygoing character. He never failed
to wake up early, in good humor, and then he would tune
the radio into a station playing good music and brew coffee
for the two of us. I'd join him in the kitchen a little later,
ready to listen to his stories and take notes.

When Highway first began to recount his stories to me,
I thought he was a compulsive liar. But then, living with
him, I realized that it had less to do with lying than surpassing the truth. Highway was one of those vast, eternal
spirits. His presence was at times menacing—not because
he was a real threat to anyone, but because, in comparison
with his ferocious freedom, all the parameters we nor-
mally use to measure our actions seem trivial. Highway

had more life in him than the usual man. Even now, after his death, there are people who think they catch a glimpse of him speeding past, gravitating toward some place or other, always mounted on the bicycle he acquired at the Gower Bicycle Pavilion outside the juice factory [figure 1]. El Perro always says that, on certain mornings, at first light, he can be seen on the top of one of the hills delimiting the scooped-out basin of this wasteland.

I transcribed his stories, and my old roommates printed them in small chapbooks on their press at the Rincón Cultural [figure 2]. Highway never saw them, but I'm sure he would have felt proud. In exchange for my work as a transcriber, Highway not only gave me board and lodging, but also an education. He took me for daily walks or bicycle rides around the streets of Ecatepec, as he was convinced that, one day, I could become the first tour guide in the area. Initially, the idea seemed foolish. If there is a physical materialization of nothingness in this world, it is Ecatepec de Morelos. But with time, I have come to believe that in this case, as with almost everything else, Highway was right. Through his stories, Ecatepec became habitable for me, so perhaps one day, if I tell those stories, it will become a place that others visit.

On the day we met, after picking up my few belongings from the apartment I shared with Darling and Understanding, we cycled to Highway's house on Disneylandia [figures 3 and 4]. The first place we went to on entering the grounds was his warehouse. He ushered me in as if we were entering some kind of temple. Highway moved slowly around the space, in silence, the indented trace of a toothless smile on his face. I followed a few steps behind him. Pointing to empty corners, he described objects, none of which were actually there: collections of teeth, of course, but also antique maps, car parts, Russian dolls, newspapers in every imaginable language, old coins, nails, bicycles, bells, doors, belts, sweaters, stones, sewing machines. He gave me a febrile tour of what he called his grand collection of collectibles. It's hard to say if those were sad or luminous moments.

Highway had once possessed an unimaginably diverse and rich collection. He was a man who truly loved material objects. And his love for them went beyond their real, material worth; for him, their value lay in that thing that, in some way, they silently enclosed. From a very early age, he had followed his impulse to meticulously collect everything he thought collectible, from coins he found on the sidewalk and buttons that fell off his schoolmates' shirts, to his father's nails and his mother's hair.

Late, but not too late, when he was forty-two, he discovered his true vocation in auctioneering. At that time he had been living with Flaca for a couple of years, and his son Siddhartha was still a dribbling infant. His whole life was ahead of him. But when Highway went to the United States with a grant to do an advanced course in auctioneering, Flaca left him. During his absence, the lady had met a recalcitrantly Catholic man from Yucatán of her own social class, and had moved in with him, taking Siddhartha with her. She died a few years later, but, in her will, she had laid out that Siddhartha should be raised by his stepfather. I imagine that Highway did not know enough about the law to realize that Flaca's testamentary disposition had no legal value whatsoever. It is my impression that Highway never recovered from the blow all this entailed, although he did have sufficient emotional resources to set aside the pain.

Despite all his training and innate talent for the art of auctioneering, when he returned to Mexico, Highway had, in fact, little luck in the profession. He took out a loan to buy a small plot in the neighborhood where he was born and built a colorful but almost uninhabitable house in Calle Disneylandia. This was Highway's home for more than two decades. Next to the house, Highway constructed a warehouse, above which he placed a placard he had custom made, saying: Oklahoma-Van Dyke Auction House.

Highway remained in his house, practically in a form of self-imposed exile, for the two following years. He only went out to buy tinned food at the corner shop, and a variety of objects in the yard belonging to the famous junk collector Jorge Ibargüengoitia [figure 5]. Every week, Highway would buy, exchange, or scavenge objects that caught his eye and, on some Sundays, organized private auctions in his house. But these forays were never completely formalized. The Sunday auctions were attended, if at all, by morbidly curious neighbors, vagabonds, and drunks. No one bought anything, so the warehouse gradually filled up with useless objects. This must have depressed Highway more than he himself knew.

Time passed, and one day a well-meaning neighbor on Disneylandia, Carlos Velázquez, contacted Siddhartha to say that Highway's "popcorn had popped." He was on his last legs, so to speak. Apparently, he no longer left the house for either food or objects. Sometimes he sat in the sun in an Acapulco chair placed outside the front door of the house. He would spend long hours there, motionless, staring into space or, occasionally, polishing some item of his collection with a cloth. According to another neighbor, Laia Jufresa, Highway had a moribund, almost cadaverous look: "His eyes were like a pair of bare lightbulbs, the white fluorescent kind." His days were numbered.

Siddhartha, an ambitious rat of the worst type, saw this as an opportunity to get hold of his father's collection, not so much because he thought it valuable, but because he thought it folkloric enough to make a good statement. Like most curators, he too wanted to have work of his own—and what better place to start than this? Knowing he would get nowhere on his own, he resolved to talk to the local priest. He suggested holding an auction, the revenues of which would benefit the church to a reasonable percentage. When he in turn heard of Highway's plight, Father Luigi Amara, of Saint Apolonia Church, saw an opportunity to kill two birds with one stone: raising funds and raising funds. He paid a visit to Highway one morning and proposed that they undertake a "joint auction." They shook on it.

A few days before the auction, Siddhartha handed Father Luigi a will for Highway to sign, in which it was stated that our hero would bequeath his whole collection of collectibles to his son. Highway signed the document without even reading it on the morning of the auction, while waiting for his cue in the church sacristy. I will never know for certain if he realized that, with that signature, he was handing over his whole life to Siddhartha. But after so much time mulling it over, my impression is that he somehow did. That would also explain the elegant irony with which Highway, once all the lots had been auctioned, looked Siddhartha straight in the eyes and asked, Who will open the bidding for me and my teeth?

Indeed, on the day before the morning when we first met, Highway and his teeth had been bought in an auction at a bargain price by his son Siddhartha Sánchez Tostado. There are various versions of what happened next. One goes that, after the auction, Siddhartha pumped him full of narcotics, and, when poor Highway fell into a deep, indefinitely long sleep, he took him to a dental dispensary where a pair of doctors removed his precious teeth. Another version says that when the auction was over, the father and son went to a cantina to settle scores, and, at the height of their drunken binge, while Siddhartha was trying to haul his father back to the car, Highway hit the tarmac so often that he simply lost the teeth. It seems unlikely. Although Highway always refused to tell me which of the two accounts of that day was true, perhaps simply because he had no clear memory of it, I think that the first version is the correct one: it was those sinister doctors who, on the orders of the even more fiendish Siddhartha, removed his teeth.

What is completely certain, as there is videotaped evidence to prove it, is that on the evening of the day of the auction, Siddhartha deposited his father in one of the salons in the Jumex art gallery. To be exact, Siddhartha dumped

Highway in a room, on the four walls of which were a video-installation showing four clowns observing the viewer with a complete lack of interest, only periodically blinking or sighing—a somewhat frightening but effective piece by the well-known artist Ugo Rondinone [figure 6]. After abandoning his father in front of Rondinone's clown installation, Siddhartha went to the room where the gallery's audiovisual security equipment was housed and proceeded to hold a remote conversation with his father through one of the loudspeaker systems. Conversation is one way of putting it: Siddhartha did his level best to torture and torment his father, and recorded it, probably for future use. He commissioned him to run a series of whimsical errands, such as finding monographs on the Russian Revolution and a white vw. But our local hero was made of sterner stuff. When the unbreakable Highway was finally able to summon up sufficient energy to leave the "room of ghosts," as he often referred to the place when recounting the anecdote, he mounted a bicycle and pedaled off into the sunrise along that now legendary street, Sonora Oriente, where our paths luckily crossed.

The next few days, after discovering that he'd lost everything, were difficult ones for Highway. He fell into a solemn silence, which he only eventually broke to say, "I think I've become a terrible person. In fact, I've become a reptile. Do you know that reptiles are stupid because almost their entire brain capacity is used to feel fear?" I urged him to get temporary dentures so he could start eating properly, and we could begin the transcription of his dental autobiography. Though he resisted at first, he finally consented, and we got down to work.

But Highway still had not fully recovered, and he existed in a kind of gray haze. Around those same days, he joined motu proprio the Serenity Group of Neurotics Anonymous, in Calle Pensadores Mexicanos, next door to the El Buho firearm repair workshop [figure 7]. His four weeks with the Serenity Group ended first badly and then well. Badly, because the first meetings left Highway convinced that he was a sick man, which he was not, and he was almost convinced to lock himself in a Catholic monastery. But well, because in his second week there, he met a veteran union boss, La Elvis, who, after hearing Highway's story during his third session with the group, persuaded him that he wasn't the least neurotic, but was in fact an honorable man, mentally and emotionally sound, whose bastard of a brat of a son had dispossessed him of what was rightfully his. She told him that she had seen a mound of teeth displayed in a gallery next to the juice factory, as if it was someone's work of art, and urged him to take action. Highway felt vindicated.

The following day we went to the gallery in the factory and took back what rightfully belonged to him, plus a few extra objects, which we thought we could sell at some future auction. We never did get far with the idea of that future auction, but Highway found and kept his teeth, and had them fit into a denture by his old friend Luis Felipe Fabre. Eventually, he thought, when he had amassed enough money, he would have them implanted individually. But for the time being, he just wore the denture as the mood took him. That is to say, sometimes in, sometimes out.

With his new teeth, Highway recovered his will to live his final months in peace. Every night, we had "Education of the Voragine Artist" sessions in the neighborhood bars. We particularly took a liking to one called Secret of Night [figure 8], where we met a young singer-songwriter called Juan Cirerol, with whom Highway performed for a few weeks, every night. I saw them the night they did a, frankly inspired, duet of Johnny Cash's classic "Highwayman," followed by Cirerol's now famous "Metanfeta." When the bar was starting to close, the owner would let Highway auction his stories. It was at Secret of Night that Highway finally put into practice the now full-fledged theory of his famous allegoric method, where it is not objects that are sold, but the stories that give them value and meaning. The allegorics were, according to Highway, "postcapitalist, radical recycling auctions that would save the world from its existential condition as the garbage can of history."

In his final performances, Highway, who was by no means lacking in ingenuity, learned to take advantage of the moments when his teeth slipped from his control to take them out altogether. He would hold them between his fingers, like the castanets they use for flamenco dancing and, depending on the occasion, make them speak or chant and tell fascinating stories of the lost objects that had once formed part of his collectibles. Increasing numbers of people came to see him and were enthralled by the spectacle of Highway's now-you-see-'em-now-you-don't dentures and the stories he told and sold with them.

He always began in roughly the same way: My name is Highway, and I'm the best auctioneer in the world. I can imitate Janis Joplin after two rums. I can stand an egg upright on a table, the way Christopher Columbus did in the famous anecdote. I can interpret Chinese fortune cookies. I know how to count to eight in Japanese: ichi, ni, san, shi, go, roku, shichi, hachi. I can float on my back.

Highway died in the Buenos Días Motel, next door to the bar, and in the company of three gorgeous ladies, after conducting an allegoric auction that finished, as an encore, with an imitation of Janis Joplin singing "Mercedes Benz." I received a call from the concierge the morning of his death and immediately went over there, with El Perro. We honored his last request, and scattered his ashes at the feet of the fiberglass dinosaurs in the median strip of a street in Pachuca, the Beautiful Windy City [figure 9]. I kept my word, and in the months that followed put together his dental autobiography. El Perro made sure Highway's son got the note that we found on the night table next to his deathbed, under the glass of water where he soaked his dentures:

> I'm sorry I got you into trouble,
> and that you're in prison,
> and that I wasn't the best of fathers.
> I also didn't get round to finding
> all the things you requested.
> But here are my teeth,

and your glass of water.
You can also keep
all my collectibles, and
the Marylin Monroe teeth,
which were false anyway.

1. GOWER BICYCLE PAVILION,
© FRANCISCO KOCHEN

Every time I see an adult on a bicycle,
I no longer despair for the future of the human race.

—H. G. WELLS

2. EL RINCÓN CULTURAL, © JAVIER RIVERO AND EL PERRO

My notebooks. So sadly full, this one with impotence, the other with empty, pointless waiting. The most difficult of waits, the most painful: the wait for oneself. If I were to write something in it, it would be the confession that I too have been waiting for myself for a long time, and I haven't turned up.

——JOSEFINA VICENS

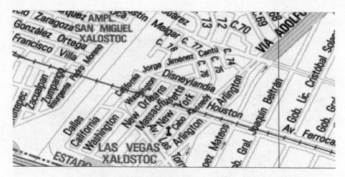

3. DISNEYLANDIA, © GUÍA ROJI

Objects in themselves disagreeable or indifferent
often please in the imitation . . .

—WILLIAM HAZLITT

4. HIGHWAY'S HOUSE, © VALERIA LUISELLI

Disneyland is presented as imaginary in order to
make us believe that the rest is real.

——JEAN BAUDRILLARD

5. ECATEPEC JUNKYARD,
© JAVIER RIVERO AND EL PERRO

The Spanish language is an old wedding dress that is handed
down to us by our ancestors, and which we are obliged to
preserve intact . . . but antique wedding dresses are only good for
putting on to see ourselves as skeletons. It's much better to cut
them up for shirts than to keep them in mothballs.

—JORGE IBARGÜENGOITIA

6. UGO RONDINONE, *WHERE DO WE GO FROM HERE,*
© LA COLECCIÓN JUMEX, MÉXICO

Fancioulle made me see that the intoxicating powers of Art are more
effective than any others for shrouding the terrors of the abyss; that
genius can represent a comedy while standing on the edge of the
tomb, with a joy that prevents it from seeing that tomb, lost as it is in
a Paradise, which refuses to admit any idea of death and destruction.

——CHARLES BAUDELAIRE

7. NEUROTICS ANON. & GUN REPAIRS,
© JAVIER RIVERO AND EL PERRO

Neurasthenia / is a gift that came to me with my earliest work.

—RUBÉN DARÍO

8. SECRET OF NIGHT,
© JAVIER RIVERO AND EL PERRO

Originality is nothing more than judicious imitation;
the most original writers borrowed from each other.

—VOLTAIRE

9. PACHUCA MEDIAN STRIP &
FIBERGLASS DINOSAURS,
© EL PULQUE

You take nothing with you when you go.
—JOSÉ MARÍA NAPOLEÓN

BOOK VII

The Chronologic

BY CHRISTINA MACSWEENEY

1938 *President Lázao Cárdenas announces the nationalization of Mexico's petroleum reserves.*

MAY 7, 1945 *War ends in Europe.*

1945 *Bertrand Russell's* A History of Western Philosophy *is published.*

Ca 1945

Gustavo Sánchez Sánchez, better known as "Highway," is born in Pachuca, the Beautiful Windy City.
His family moves to Ecatepec de Morelos.

1940 *Production at the United States Smelting, Refining & Mining Company in Pachuca declines, causing many residents to leave in search of employment.*

CA 1945 *Paul Klee's painting* Angelus Novus *passes into the care of Theodor Adorno after its owner, Walter Benjamin, commits suicide in Portbou.*

1945 *Fifty years since Mr. Hoopdriver set out on a cycling tour of southeast England in H. G. Wells's* The Wheels of Chance.

1950 *Virginia Woolf's essay "Gas,"*
which details her experience of having
several teeth extracted in 1922 and 1923, is
published in The Captain's Death Bed
and Other Essays.

1948 *Centennial of the birth of German*
logician and philosopher Gottlob Frege.

1954 *Author Francisco Goldman is born in Boston, Massachusetts.*

1956 *Julio Cortázar meditates on the metamorphosis of an axolotl in the Jardin des Plantes, Paris, in his short story "Axolotl."*

Ca 1953

Highway starts his first job in Rubén Darío's newspaper stand and begins a collection of straws.

1951 Siddhartha *by Hermann Hesse is first published in the United States and later helps inspire the hippie generation.*

1955 *Fifty years since Miguel de Unamuno, upon receiving the Gran Cruz de Alfonso X, said to Alfonso XIII, "I am honored, Your Majesty, to receive this cross, which I so justly deserve."*

1957 *Penguin publishes Robert Graves's translations of Suetonius's* The Twelve Caesars.

1962 *Centennial of the publication of the first fifty prose poems of* Le Spleen de París *by Charles Baudelaire, which includes an account of the heroic death of the court jester Fancioulle.*

1962 *In her biography of Robert de Montesquiou, Cornelia Otis Skinner reports that Marcel Proust often copied Montesquiou's laugh and his habit of not showing his teeth.*

1965 *Work begins on the construction of Mexico's first Volkswagen plant.*

1962 *The first Scribe notebooks are manufactured in Mexico.*

1966 *Five hundred fifty years ago, Poggio Bracciolini discovered an edition of Quintilian's* Institutio Oratoria *in an old tower at the Abbey of St. Gall in Switzerland.*

1967 *U.S. country singer Leroy Van Dyke stars in the film* What Am I Bid?

1968 *Possibly the fiftieth anniversary of the invention of the Chinese fortune cookie by Donald Lau in Los Angeles.*

OCTOBER 12, 1968 *The Olympic Games open in Mexico.*

1968 *Multimedia artist Doug Aitken is born in Redondo Beach, California.*

1966

Highway is employed as a security guard at the Júmex factory in Ecatepec de Morelos.
He continues collecting.

1967 *The Beatles release* Sgt. Pepper's Lonely Hearts Club Band *with an album sleeve designed by Peter Blake and Jann Haworth.*

1967 *Sol LeWitt's "Paragraphs on Conceptual Art" is published in* Artforum.

1967 *The 150th anniversary of the publication of* The Round Table, *a collection of essays by William Hazlitt.*

OCTOBER 2, 1968 *Protesting students are massacred in Tlatelolco Square, Mexico City.*

1970 *Mexican American author and editor David Miklos is born in San Antonio, Texas.*

1971 *Four hundred years since Michel de Montaigne, weary of active life, retired to his father's château at age thirty-seven.*

1971 *Essayist, poet, and editor Luigi Amara is born in Mexico City.*

1971 *Miguel Calderón, the enfant terrible of Mexican art, is born in Mexico City.*

1973 *Jorge Luis Borges resigns as director of the Biblioteca Nacional in Buenos Aires after being awarded the first Premio Internacional Alfonso Reyes.*

1973 *Centennial of the publication of John Stuart Mill's autobiography, which includes comments on how Quintilian influenced his thinking.*

JULY 2, 1976 *Saigon renamed Ho Chi Minh City.*

1976 *The Voltaire Foundation is inaugurated at the University of Oxford.*

1978 *Carlos Velázquez, writer of norteña literature, is born in Coahuila, Mexico.*

EARLY 1970s *Spanish author Enrique Vila-Matas first reads about the artist Raymond Roussel in the works of Marcel Duchamp.*

1970 *Bicentennial of the first scholarly translation of Plutarch's Parallel Lives from the original Greek into English.*

OCTOBER 1, 1970 *Janis Joplin records "Mercedes Benz" at the Sunset Sound recording studio in Los Angeles.*

1971 *Approximately 1,600 years since a young Augustine of Hippo prayed, "Grant me chastity and continence, but not yet."*

1971 *Part I of Allan Kaprow's "The Education of the Un-Artist" is published in Art News 69. In 2011, Mexican author and poet Daniel Saldaña París uploads Kaprow's essay to Scribd.*

1971 *Three-dimensional artist Fernando Ortega is born in Mexico City.*

1974 *Poet, essayist, and editor Luis Felipe Fabre is born in Mexico City: Pisces, Libra ascendant, moon in Aries.*

1975–1982 *Fifty years since the serial-format publication of Aleksandr Sergeyevich Pushkin's novel in verse, Eugene Onegin.*

1976 *The 350th anniversary of the death of Francis Bacon, the father of empiricism, who suffered pneumonia after conducting an experiment on the effects of freezing meat, which involved stuffing a fowl with snow.*

1982 *Bicentennial of the publication of Jean-Jacques Rousseau's* Les rêveries du promeneur solitaire.

1982 *In the introduction to a collection of stories by Robert Walser, Susan Sontag compares Walser's prose to the art of Paul Klee.*

APRIL 15, 1980 *Tens of thousands join Jean-Paul Sartre's funeral precession to his burial plot in Montparnasse.*

Ca 1980

Highway is promoted to Crisis Manager.
He begins collecting courses.

1980 *Pablo Duarte, editor of the Letras Libres website, is born in Mexico City.*

1981 *An asteroid is discovered and named 3453 Dostoevsky.*

1982 *In* Wittgenstein on Rules and Private Language, *Saul Kripke introduces Kripkenstein, a fictional character who holds views based on Wittgenstein's writings.*

1983 *Mexican short-story writer, novelist, and playwright Jorge Ibargüengoitia is buried in Antillón Park beneath a plaque that reads: "Here lies Jorge Ibargüengoitia, in the park of his great-grandfather who fought against the French."*

JUNE 25, 1984 *Michel Foucault dies at age fifty-seven in the Pitié-Salpêtrière Hospital in Paris.*

1984

Highway marries Flaca.

1983 *Five hundredth anniversary of the publication of Jacobus de Voragine's Golden Legend, Caxton edition, which recounts the lives of the saints.*

1984 *Mexican singer José María Napoleón, often called the poet of melody, releases the single "Nunca cambies."*

SEPTEMBER 19, 1985 *Massive earthquake under Mexico City leaves at least ten thousand people dead.*

1986 *Jean Baudrillard writes* America, *an account of his travels in the United States.*

September 19, 1985

Siddhartha Sánchez Tostado is born.

SEPTEMBER 1985 *"Highwayman" is number one on the U.S. country music charts.*

1985 *Carlos Fuentes publishes* Gringo viejo.

JUNE 8, 1987 *Singer-songwriter Juan Cirerol—Mexico's Johnny Cash—is born in Mexicali. His second album includes the track "Clonazepam Blues."*

1987 *Mexican writer Mario Bellatin travels to Cuba to study screenwriting.*

1986–1987

Highway attends an auctioneering course given by Master Oklahoma.
He meets Leroy Van Dyke at the Missouri Auction School.
Flaca leaves Highway, taking Siddhartha with her.

1987 *Mexican author Guillermo Fadanelli lives in Berlin for a year and is surprised to find that the beer is not served cold.*

JULY 1988 *Centennial of the first-edition publication of Rubén Darío's* Azul.

1989 *Josefina Vicens's short story "Petrita" is published posthumously. The story is based on a painting entitled* La niña muerta, *which was given to Vicens by the artist Juan Soriano.*

1988–2000

Highway becomes a successful auctioneer and travels widely. He begins to develop his allegoric auctioning method.

1989 *A Yoko Ono retrospective is held at a Whitney Museum branch.*

1991 *The 650th anniversary of the appointment of Petrarch as the first poet laureate since the classical era.*

1992 *Sam Durant has his first solo exhibition at the Bliss Gallery in Pasadena.*

1995 *Three hundredth anniversary of the death of Sor Juana Inés de la Cruz, whose writings are said to show the influence of the classical rhetoric of Aristotle, Quintilian, and Plato.*

1991 *Serpent's Tail publishes Susan Bassnett's translation of Margo Glantz's* The Family Tree: An Illustrated Novel *in the United Kingdom.*

AUGUST 3, 1992 *Five hundred years since Christopher Columbus set out to find a westward passage to the Orient and accidentally discovered the Caribbean islands.*

1998 *Bicentennial of the publication of Charles Lamb's poem "The Old Familiar Faces," in which describes his "day of horrors."*

CA 1998 *Fifteen-year-old Valeria Luiselli buys a copy of Sergio Pitol's* Vals de mefisto *in a bookstore in San Cristóbal de las Casas and imagines him to be a dead Eastern European or Russian writer.*

OCTOBER 27 AND 28, 1999
Christie's auctions Marilyn Monroe's personal property, including a collection of eleven assorted Mexican soda glass tumblers.

2000 *Approximately 2,400 years since the Greek dramatist Euripides, who depicted mythical characters as ordinary people, retired to a cave on the island of Salamis to write his tragedies.*

DECEMBER 3, 2001 *Mexican experimental short-story writer Juan José Arreola dies.*

2002 *The number of undocumented Mexicans living in the United States is estimated to be 5.3 million.*

2002 *Visual artist Terence Gower installs Bicycle Pavilion in the grounds of the Fundación/Colección Júmex in Ecatepec, Mexico City.*

2003 *Olafur Eliasson represents Denmark in the Venice Biennale.*

2004 *Short-story writer and essayist Vivian Abenshushan is inspired by a piece of stencil art in Buenos Aires that reads, "Kill your boss: resign."*

Ca 2000

Highway buys Marilyn Monroe's teeth in an auction in Miami.

2000 *Approximately three thousand years since Cadmus, son of Telephassa, sowed a dragon's tooth and was surprised to see armed warriors spring from the earth.*

2000 *The United Nations launches its eight Millennium Development Goals to be achieved by 2015.*

2002 *The 150th anniversary of the death of Nikolai Vasilievich Gogol.*

2002 *Approximately 1,900 years since Tacitus wrote Dialogus de oratoribus.*

2004 *Posthumous publication of Uruguayan author Mario Levrero's La novela luminosa, which includes a 450-page prologue recounting how the writer spent the grant awarded to him by the Guggenheim Foundation.*

2005 One hundred years since the Russian absurdist writer Daniil Kharms was born twice; the author claims that his father and the midwife tried to push him back into the womb when he appeared four months prematurely.

2006 Chilean writer Alejandro Zambra's novel Bonsái is published in Spain by Anagrama.

2007 Mexican critic Guillermo Sheridan begins to write his blog El minutario, hosted by Letras Libres.

2007 Yuri Herrera-Gutiérrez becomes editor of the literary magazine El perro.

2009 El Dinoparque opens in the Museo El Rehilete in Pachuca.

2010 Author Carlos Yushimito is described by Granta as "a Peruvian of Japanese forbears who lives in Providence, Rhode Island, and who writes about Brazil."

2009 Sexto Piso publishes Emiliano Monge's novel Morirse de memoria.

2010 At age twenty-seven, while in Wisconsin, Mexican writer Laia Jufresa learns how to ride a bicycle.

2001–2010

Highway buys a plot on Calle Disneylandia and lives in seclusion. He continues to collect local memorabilia.

2005 One hundredth anniversary of the publication of G. K. Chesterton's essay "A Piece of Chalk."

OCTOBER 13, 2006 Two hundred years since German philosopher Georg Wilhelm Friedrich Hegel saw Napoléon ride through the streets of Jena.

2006 El buscador de cabezas, by Guadalajara-born Antonio Ortuño, is selected as the best debut novel of the year by the newspaper Reforma.

2007 Mexican telecoms magnate Carlos Slim is reported to be the world's richest man.

2008 In his essay "El arte de vivir en arte," Argentine writer and critic Alan Pauls states that fiction can be understood as "a map based on coincidences and divergences."

JULY 29, 2010 Winston Churchill's "world saving" teeth are sold for £15,200 in auction in Norfolk, England.

2010 Rubén Gallo publishes Freud's Mexico: Into the Wilds of Psychoanalysis.

2010 Mexican artist Damián Ortega creates a new artwork every day for a month for his exhibition at the Barbican Art Gallery.

2011 *Conceptual artist Abraham Cruzvillegas installs* Autoconstrucción, *which contains sheep, shit, and clumps of hair, at the Tate Modern.*

2012 *Christie's sells Andy Warhol's 1984 screen print* Saint Apollonia: one plate *at auction.*

APRIL 27, 2012 *David Weiss, half of the artistic duo Fischli/Weiss, dies at age sixty-six.*

JUNE 2012 *Javier Rivero posts a photograph with the caption "Kitty proofreading Jean-Paul Sartre" on his blog,* Writers and Kitties.

2011–2013

Parabolic auction takes place at Saint Apolonia Church.

Highway spends the night in the "room of ghosts."

He meets would-be writer Jacobo de Voragine and proposes that Jacobo write his dental autobiography.

Highway recovers his teeth.

NOVEMBER 2011 *The Manhattan Guggenheim Museum describes the Italian hyperrealist artist Maurizio Cattelan as a provocateur and prankster.*

MARCH 2011 *The murder of poet Javier Sicilia's son leads to mass protests throughout Mexico against drug-related violence.*

2011 *Article entitled "The Musical Brain" by prolific Argentine writer César Aira appears in* The New Yorker.

2012 *Julián Herbert wins the Premio Jaén de Novela Inédita for the autobiographical novel* Canción de tumba, *which recounts the death of his mother—a former prostitute—from leukemia.*

2013 *Álvaro Enrigue's novel* Muerte súbita *wins the Premio Herralde de Novela.*

2012 *Mexican poet, essayist, and translator Tedi López Mill publishes her collection of poems* El libro de las explicaciones.

2013 *A red fish called Oblomov dies of some kind of depression in Guadalupe Nettel's collection of short stories* El matrimonio de los peces rojos.

2013

Highway dies in the Buenos Días Motel after conducting an allegoric auction in Secret of Night.

2012 *Paula Abramo publishes her collection of poems,* Fiat Lux.

MARCH 2012 *New York-based artist Ugo Rondinone curates an exhibition that includes Hans Schärer's* Madonna, *in which the teeth are replaced by yellowing pebbles.*

APRIL 8, 2013 *The Fundación/ Colección Júmex opens its exhibition* El cazador y la fábrica.

2013 *A two-Euro coin is minted to celebrate the 2,400th anniversary of the foundation of Plato's Academy.*

Afterword

THIS BOOK IS THE RESULT OF SEVERAL COLLABORA-
tions. In January 2013, I was commissioned to write a
work of fiction for the catalog of *The Hunter and the Factory,*
an exhibition curated by Magalí Arriola and Juan Gaitán at
Galería Jumex, a gallery located in the marginalized, waste-
land-like neighborhood of Ecatepec outside Mexico City.
The idea behind the exhibition, and my commission, was
to reflect upon the bridges—or the lack thereof—between
the featured artwork, the gallery, and the larger context of
which the gallery formed part.

The Jumex Collection, one of the most important contemporary art collections in the world, is funded by Grupo
Jumex—a juice factory. There is, naturally, a gap between
the two worlds: gallery and factory, artists and workers, artwork and juice. How could I link the two distant but neigh-
boring worlds, and could literature play a mediating role?
I decided to write tangentially—even allegorically—about
the art world, and to focus on the life of the factory. I also
decided to write not so much *about* but *for* the factory workers, suggesting a procedure that seemed appropriate to this
end.

In mid-nineteenth century Cuba, the strange métier of "tobacco reader" was invented. The idea is attributed to Nicolás Azcárate, a journalist and active abolitionist, who put it into practice in a cigar factory. In order to reduce the tedium of repetitive labor, a tobacco reader would read aloud to the other workers while they made the cigars. Emile Zola and Victor Hugo were among the favorites, though lofty volumes of Spanish history were also read. The practice spread to other Latin American countries but disappeared in the twentieth century. In Cuba, however, tobacco readers are still common. Around the same time this practice emerged, the modern serial novel was also invented. In 1836, Balzac's *La Vieille Fille* was published in France, and Dickens's *The Pickwick Papers* was published in England. Distributed as affordable, serialized chapbooks, they reached an audience not traditionally accustomed to reading fiction. I realized I could combine these two literary devices that had once proven adequate in contexts not too different from the one I was facing. In order to pay tribute to and learn from these reading and publishing practices, I decided to write a novel in installments for the workers, who could then read it out loud in the factory.

The Jumex team was supportive and enthusiastic, and set up a space and the necessary conditions for the readings to take place. I wrote the first installment, which was printed as very low-budget, simple chapbooks that were distributed to the workers. A few workers became interested, and the curatorial assistant, Lorena Moreno, helped form and moderate a small reading club that met each week to read and discuss the pieces. I started sending new installments each week; the team at the Jumex Foundation printed the chapbooks and distributed them. With everyone's consent, the reading sessions were recorded and sent back to me in New York. I would listen to them, taking note of the workers' comments, criticisms, and especially their informal talk after the reading and discussion. I'd then write the next installment, send it back to them, and so on. They never saw me; I never saw them. I heard them, and they read me. Two members of the Jumex team, Javier Rivero and El Perro, also helped me take and collect pictures of the artwork, the gallery, and the neighborhood, which enabled me, virtually at least, to move around and explore the spaces I was writing about. The formula, if there was one, would be something like Dickens + MP3 ÷ Balzac + JPEG. With the last installment, I also sent the workers an MP3 recording of my voice, thanking them for their time and input. I had been writing under the pseudonym Gustavo Sánchez Sánchez, and I thought it was important to close the circle of intimacy we had created by letting them hear my real voice. Their reaction to my spoken voice was probably similar to my reaction when, months later, two of the workers appeared at the book launch in Mexico City at the Museo de Arte Carrillo Gil. That is when the circle really closed.

Many of the stories told in this book come from the workers' personal accounts—though names, places, and details are modified. The discussions between the workers also directed the course of the narrative, pushing me to reflect upon old questions from a new perspective: How do art objects acquire value not only within the specialized market for art consumption, but also outside its (more or less) well-defined boundaries? How does distancing an object or name from its context in a gallery, museum, or literary pantheon—a *reverse* Duchampian procedure—affect its meaning and interpretation? How do discourse, narrative, and authorial signatures or names modify the way we perceive artwork and literary texts? The result of these shared concerns is this collective "novel-essay" about the production of value and meaning in contemporary art and literature.

For their input and dedication, I would like to thank many people, but more than anyone, I'd like to thank the factory workers who read and somehow wrote this story with me: Evelyn Ángeles Quintana, Abril Velázquez Romero, Tania García Montalva, Marco Antonio Bello, Eduardo González, Ernestina Martínez, Patricia Méndez Cortés, Julio Cesar Velarde Mejía, and David León Alcalá.

Finally, I should say that from the initial installments read by the workers in the factory to this final version of the book in English, many things have changed. In fact, the Spanish book is also different from the English one—as has been the case with my previous books, which I revise and rewrite so thoroughly in English that I prefer to conceive of them as versions rather than translations. This English edition, moreover, includes an extra "chapbook" written entirely by my translator, Christina MacSweeney. Her Chronologic is a map, an index, and a glossary for the book, which both destabilizes the obsolete dictum of the translator's invisibility and suggests a new way of engaging with translation; one that neither relies on bringing the writer closer to the reader—by simplifying and glossing the translated text—nor on bringing the reader closer to the writer—by means of rendering the text into a kind of "foreign English." This book began as a collaboration, and I like to think of it as an ongoing one, where every new layer modifies the entire content completely.

ABOUT THE TRANSLATOR

CHRISTINA MACSWEENEY has an MA in literary translation from the University of East Anglia and specializes in Latin American fiction. Her translations have previously appeared in a variety of online sites and literary magazines. She has also translated Valeria Luiselli's novel, *Faces in the Crowd,* and essay collection, *Sidewalks.*

The Story of My Teeth contains references to many texts, and in most cases these are creatively interpreted, paraphrased, or have been altered slightly through multiple translations.

Pg. 12: Gaius Suetonius Tranquillus quote from *The Twelve Caesars,* translated by Robert Graves. Penguin Books, 1957.

Pg. 18: Jean Baudrillard quote from *America,* translated by Chris Turner. Verso, 1989.

Pg. 25: Cervantes.

Pg. 41: Michel Foucault quote from "The Lives of Infamous Men" in *Power: Essential Works of Foucault 1954–1984, Volume 3,* translated by Robert Hurley. The New Press, 2001.

Pg. 48: Michel de Montaigne quote from "Of Experience."

Pg. 50: Charles Lamb quote from *The Life, Letters and Writings of Charles Lamb Volume II.*

Pg. 51: G. K. Chesterton quote from "The Appetite of Earth" in *Alarms and Discursions.* Dodd, Mead and Company, 1911.

Pg. 65: Marcel Proust quote from *Remembrance of Things Past: Swann's Way,* translated by C. K. Scott Montcrieff. Henry Bolt, 1922.

Pg. 80: Danill Kharms quote based on excerpt from *Today I Wrote Nothing: The Selected Writings of Daniil Kharms.* Ardis Publishers, 2007.

Pg. 85: Based on a line from Shakespeare's *Much Ado About Nothing*.

Pg. 107: Based on sayings by Vince Lombardi, Cervantes, and unattributed Latin, Chinese, and Spanish proverbs.

Pg. 125: Walter Benjamin quote based on excerpt from "Theses on the Philosophy of History" in *Illuminations*. Schocken Books, 1968.

Keep in touch with
Granta Books:

Visit grantabooks.com to discover more.

GRANTA

Also by Valeria Luiselli and published by Granta Books
www.grantabooks.com

SIDEWALKS

Evocative, erudite and consistently surprising, these narrative
essays explore the places – real and imagined – that shape
our lives. We follow Valeria Luiselli as she cycles around
Mexico City, shares a cigarette with the night porter in her
Harlem apartment and hunts down a poet's tomb in Venice.
Each location sparks Luiselli's nimble curiosity and prompts
imaginative reflections and inventions on topics as varied as
the fluidity of identity, the elusiveness of words that can't be
translated, the competing methods of arranging a bookcase,
and the way that city-dwellers evade eye-contact with
their neighbours while spying on their lives.

'Vivid and shrewd' *TLS*

'Lucidly intelligent' *Daily Telegraph*

'All year I've been telling people to read Luiselli's glancing,
subtle essays, in *Sidewalks*'
Adam Thirlwell, Books of the Year 2013, *TLS*

'A wonderful contribution to the long tradition by which
authors re-imagine their cities as dream-like spaces' *LA Times*

'Illuminating and delightful' *Flavourwire*

FACES IN THE CROWD

In the heart of Mexico City, a young mother begins a novel
about her days in New York and her obsession with an
obscure poet of the Harlem Renaissance. As she writes, the
decades between the author and her character blur and she
begins to be haunted by this solitary man living on the edges
of Harlem's drinking circles, troubled by his own spectral
visions of a young woman travelling the New York subway.

'Astonishingly inventive . . . Luiselli is a precociously
masterful, entirely original writer'
Francisco Goldman, author of *Say Her Name*

'*Faces in the Crowd* signals the appearance of an exciting voice
to join a new wave of Latin American writers' *Observer*

'A remarkably confident novel . . . ambitious in the ideas that
crackle through its voices, in its complex structure and the
daring intimacy of its field of vision' *Independent*

'Spare, strange and beautiful . . . an extraordinary new
literary talent' *Telegraph*

'A sexy, surreal debut' *Metro*